MONO MUTANTE

A Pedro the Water Dog Saves the Planet Primer

AVIS KALFSBEEK

Let's Keep In Touch

Find more stories, updates, and community at
www.AvisKalfsbeek.com

Yours in peaceful love of the planet,

Acknowledgments:

1100 Farm – AnimalClock.org - Benjamin Katz Creative - Brendan Kelty Trio

Burgs – Carmel Bella Farm – ConsumerNotice.org - Ghetto Gastro

Haudenosaunee Thanksgiving Address

Indigenous Seed Keepers Network

John Kempf - Lanzo del Vasto - Louise and Percy Schmeiser

Mt. Wolf - NavdanyaInternational.org - NonGMOProject.org

Project Backboard - Rowen White - Sister José Hobday

Slow Food USA - Wendell Berry

ISBN 978-1-953965-06-6 (First Edition Hardback)

ISBN 978-1-953965-07-3 (First Edition Paperback)

ISBN 978-1-953965-08-0 (Ebook)

www.AvisKalfsbeek.com

For my father Peter Charles Kalfsbeek,
my brother Charles Joseph Kalfsbeek,
third-and fourth-generation farmers,

and

Jamie D.

Foreward

Before we dive into this satirical eco-adventure, here are a few grounding truths and inspirations – seeds from which this story grew.

"We reviewed 63 epidemiological studies on exposure to pesticides and cancer risk in humans published from 2017 to 2021...Though the existing evidence has limitations, as always in science, there is sufficient evidence to implement policies and regulatory action that limit pesticide exposure in humans and, hence, further prevent a significant burden of cancers."

Exposures to pesticides and risk of cancer: Evaluation of recent epidemiological evidence in humans and paths forward, published by the International Journal of Cancer, September 2022

AVIS KALFSBEEK

"If you want to know where you would have stood on slavery before the Civil War, don't look at where you stand on slavery today. Look at where you stand on animal rights."
  Captain Paul Watson, Canadian anti-whaling activist

"As long as men massacre animals, they will kill each other. Indeed, he who sows the seeds of murder and pain cannot reap the joy of love."
  Pythagoras

"The sunflower's heart is not visible to most..."
  Hafiz

"Make a life that does not disturb the life from which it came."
  Pedro (inspired by Wendell Berry's How to Be a Poet)

CHAPTER 1

Crimson Giant Radish

(ENDANGERED)

In a modern time when many say the earth will not sustain human life, a delicate hand reaches for a bunch of lacinato kale in a row of beautiful multi-colored produce nestled in wicker bins. Tilly, a wholesome, fit, young woman with long black hair and an olive complexion, adds spinach, red and orange beets, broccoli, carrots, and three heirloom tomatoes, striped purple and red, to her basket. She wears dark teal running leggings and a hoodie that reads *One More Year.*

"These are beautiful. I bet they're Carmella's," Tilly says, holding a tomato.

"Yep. Good for your baby bump," Camas says, tossing a bag of russet potatoes into her basket with a garlic bulb and an onion. Tilly's best friend Camas is a full-figured woman in her late twenties, strong, radiant, with curly strawberry-blond hair, freckles, and a tattooed arm. Her neon running gear clashes with the calm of the produce.

Camas adds a bag of small red potatoes to her basket, then a large bag of kettle chips.

"Potatoes for dinner?" Tilly teases.

"You can never go wrong with spuds. Fries, hash browns, mashed potatoes, twice-baked potatoes, potato salad, potato soup, country fries, steak fries, waffle fries, crinkle-cut fries, shoestring fries, potato au gratin, pommes frites..."

"Pommes frites are just french fries. And you named five other types of fries."

"If I had to live on one food forever, it'd be fries."

"At least you'd be a vegetarian, but maybe diversify a little."

"Josh gives me grief too. But potatoes are full of antioxidants, Vitamin C, B6, potassium, and maganeezie."

"Manganese?"

"Yeah. It's a vitamin."

"It's a mineral," Tilly corrects. "They say potatoes have mood-boosting qualities and you're one of the happiest people I know."

"Potatoes, not Prozac, sista. I could be the poster girl for the potato!" Camas says, swinging her hips.

"Yes, you are," Tilly laughs.

"Spuds for the spiritual," Camas adds, grabbing another chip bag.

"I meditated this morning, and the Universe told me to add kale," Tilly says, tossing a bunch into her basket.

"Hey!" Camas picks it up and lays it back in her basket. "OK, I'll keep it." She shrugs.

"We're lucky to have Sandglass Natural Foods," Tilly says, looking around. "We take all this variety for granted."

They pass under a large *organic non-GMO* sign and head down the baby food aisle. Tilly inspects jars and picks out two.

"Isn't it early to buy baby food?" Camas asks, skeptical.

"I'm testing recipes. Want to taste test with me?"

"No, thank you."

They pass the refrigerators. Camas grabs a steak and a swing-top six-pack of Flensburger beer, placing them in her basket. She pops open a bottle and takes a swig. "We never camp."

Tilly grimaces.

"Are you frowning at the steak or the beer?" Camas asks.

"Both, but you can't open a beer in here."

"Our run and the salty fries talk made me thirsty," Camas says, snapping the ceramic stopper back on. "And seriously. We haven't camped in ages."

"We camped across the entire U.S. on the Great Petal Pedal Ride."

"I mean lately. Once that baby pops out, we won't be able to," Camas whines. "You'll need the baby supplies and baby food, and you'll be sleep deprived and..."

"Cam, I'll just need my breasts."

"It'll want your whole attention."

At checkout, Tilly picks up a magazine. "Ghetto Gastro is talking about food as a race issue," she says, pointing to the cover.

"Huh?"

"Here we are in this beautiful store, " Tilly gestures to her basket, "and other places have no access to healthy food."

Camas loads her potatoes, steak, and beer on the belt and tosses on a large peanut butter cup. "Let me see that?" Camas takes the magazine. "Oooh, those guys are sexy!"

"Peaceful Monday to you," says Shelly, the earth-mama cashier with dreadlocks and a nose ring. Then firmly, "No drinking in the store, Camas."

"Thanks, Shelly. Now, I know."

"I told you last time."

"You did?" Camas says innocently. Avoiding Shelley's eyes, she reads aloud, "Never forget that the agricultural power and history of farming in this country is entirely a result of Black people's labor. We don't use the term food deserts because that implies a natural occurrence of some sort. This shit is anything but natural."

Camas grabs a pie off the rack and puts it on the belt.

"They're right," Tilly says. "I won't use 'food desert' anymore. Maybe 'food wasteland' instead?"

"Food fucked?" Camas says loudly.

Customers turn to look.

"That works," Tilly says solemnly. She pays in cash.

Outside, bags in hand, Camas answers her phone. "Hello?"

Pause.

"Uh-huh. Uh-huh." Her expression shifts.

Tilly waits.

"That was my dad. My mom died."

"Oh, Camas." Tilly wraps her arms around her.

"I've inherited a farmhouse," Camas says softly.

CHAPTER 2

Macedonian Sweet Pepper

(ENDANGERED)

Jocelyn, "Joss," a petite young Black woman in copper bike shorts and a *Seed Sovereignty* tee, moves hangers from right to left in the baby section of an overstuffed thrift store. A small backpack sits snug against her back, and bob-length highlighted ringlets frame her face. She scoots through the narrow aisle with her 8-month-old son in a stroller and pulls a used BabyBjörn from the rack. She pays for it at the cash register and steps outside.

On a city bench, she threads her arms through the carrier straps, then lifts her baby to her chest with a warm smile. She snaps him inside. A city bus hisses to a stop. Joss folds the stroller swiftly and steps onto the bus.

Onboard, she pulls a wax-covered reusable bag out of her backpack and retrieves a pacifier, tucking it into her son's mouth. Her eyes shift to the window and land on a looming billboard. A bald, Mister-Clean-looking man brandishes a hunting knife over blood-red meat sliced on a stars-and-stripes-stained cutting board. Large block letters spell "The Beau Crimson Encounter."

A slight woman with long white hair walks slowly through a glowing aquamarine-colored ice cave. Perla Seruma wears a cream Icelandic sweater, jeans, boots, and a white parka. Her graceful neck is lit by the cave's eerie blue glow. She spreads a small mat, sits cross-legged, and opens a journal on her lap. Eyes closed, palms open, she breathes.

A young man in a full snow suit stands quietly nearby.

"Jón," Perla calls softly, her voice echoes against cave walls that crackle with small melting streams.

"Yes, Prime Minister?"

"Langjokull won't be here in 100 years."

"Yes, I've read that."

"Okjökull glacier is already gone. The glaciers are retreating more than an Olympic-sized pool every decade. In 200 years, they'll all be gone."

"Maybe sooner."

He offers his hand. She stands.

"They say glacier dust helps farmers, creates a carbon sink, boosts yields by thirty percent," Jón says.

"Some will say, 'See, the earth is taking care of itself,'" Perla says solemnly.

"It's a bright spot, though, isn't it?"

Perla rests her gloved hand on Jón's sleeve. "Saying glacier dust will save us is like saying our savior lies in sea sediment and we need to drain the ocean to get it."

A drop falls onto Jón's forehead. Perla reaches up and gently wipes it off.

"Takk. Prime Minister, we'd better head back. Your flight to Norway leaves at noon."

"I'm taking some seeds to the Svalbard Seed Vault. I can't be late. I'm meeting other seed Elders there."

Joss steps off the bus and enters the Culver City Food Co-op. She grabs a small basket and heads to the produce section. From her backpack, she pulls a small spectrometer, about the size of her phone, and holds it up to an heirloom tomato, then kale, apple, beet, and blueberries, glancing at her phone after each scan.

"Is it working yet, J?" asks Mr. Palak, a middle-aged man with a potbelly under his apron. He grins at her baby, looking up at him from the front pack.

"Almost, Mr. Palak."

"How does that thing work again?"

"It scans nutrient density."

"Interesting. The shoppers may like it, but some of our suppliers won't. They care more about shelf life than nutrition. Finish that up. I don't want to get in trouble."

"I'm almost done. Thanks." Joss scans a banana, bell pepper, and butternut squash, then tucks the device away. "See you soon."

"OK, see you!"

Joss adds vegetables, a fresh baguette, and hummus to her basket. Outside, the neighborhood buzzes. *Cool to Live* by DJ Cavem plays from a boombox beside a man with long gray dreads and a cattle dog in a reggae-colored bandana. She walks home past a tiny liquor store with "Grocery" in faded paint on the window. Past a wall of liquor behind bars, she scans a sad tomato and a wilted head of iceberg lettuce next to Olde English 800 and energy drinks. Her device flashes a result. She frowns.

Her son whimpers. She kisses his head. "It's OK. We'll fix this."

She scans a limp bunch of cilantro, then buys a pack of gum, and leaves.

The Icelandic Prime Minister's helicopter lifts off Langjökull glacier, soaring over Iceland's dramatic landscape. Glacial runoff thunders through the Hvítá River canyon. Steam puffs from ancient geothermal vents. Pools glow neon-blue, copper, and chocolate, glistening like sliced, polished agate.

Bright sunshine pours over time-lapse images of so-perfect-it-could-be-plastic Iowan corn. Tiny sprouts push from the earth, to shoots, to silks in thick GMO maize rows. A crop duster flies low over a cornfield, covering the crops and the field with a dust of pesticides.

A Blue Jay perches above Harvard's Countway Library Community Garden. Students and professors chat with local farmers below. The bird lands on the windowsill.

Inside, Professor Olivier Clan, constitutional law sage, stands before a slide on a large screen titled "How the Founding Fathers' Gardens Changed the Constitution."

"Rolf, why was gardening so important to the Founding Fathers?" Olivier asks.

"They believed Americans should be virtuous agrarian citizens who were connected to the land."

"And Cicily?"

Cicily straightens. "During the Constitutional Convention, delegates visited horticulturist John Bartram's garden. There, plants from all 13 states were entwined, symbolizing unity."

Chapter 3

Roundup Ready™ Corn – Zea mays l. – Maize

(GMO - Monsanto)

A flash of sunrise squeezes between a tall Engelmann spruce tree and the broad shoulder of a grizzly on a glacier-carved mountain above Sandglass. The bear paws at a cluster of morels, plucks a few stocky stems, munches the brain-textured mushrooms, then rises on her hind legs, nine feet tall. She scans the trees, then lumbers away.

Camas sings full throttle as she skims across Lake Bijou Nez in her 1950s-era atomic runabout wearing bright aqua shorts, a lime-green

sports bra, and a faded visor that reads *three island swim*. Pine trees, old cabins, and resort homes blur past.

She takes a swig of beer, tosses the empty can onto the floorboard, and eases the motor as the One More Year offices come into view above the Sandglass Rowing Club boathouse. She ties off at the dock, grabs two cloth grocery bags, and bounds up the outdoor stairs to the deck overlooking the lake, then inside.

Pedro, Tilly's curly black-haired dog, leaps from his spot beside Tilly's desk to bounce up to kiss her.

"Down, Pedro. P, down!" Camas laughs.

Pedro sniffs at the bags.

"Good morning, Sunshine. P, lie down," Tilly says.

Pedro obeys with a huff.

Camas drops into her chair across from Tilly. "Morning."

"You've been running?" Tilly asks.

"Nope."

"You're sweaty."

"It's dried sweat."

"It still counts." Tilly wrinkles her nose. "Whew, you smell funky. Like a brewery and forest floor."

"We were picking mushrooms. Josh and I hit the motherlode of morels on Celtic Peak. I figured the professional mycophiles cleared it out already, but we went off the trail, rounded a bend, and boom. Spiky honeycomb elf wonderland."

"Are you sure you weren't multi-shrooming. You're unusually expressive this morning."

"I'm clear. Well, mostly." Camas lifts a bag. "Here, these are for you and Liam."

"Thank you!" Tilly opens the bag and gasps at the bounty.

"Yes, yes," Camas says. "I gave thanks when I picked them."

"You did?"

"Well, I might have rushed."

"Camas," Tilly scolds gently, "morels are sacred."

She gathers both bags and heads to the deck. Camas and Pedro follow. Tilly sits cross-legged and turns down the edges of the bags to reveal the mushrooms. She closes her eyes. Camas follows suit. Pedro sniffs, then flops beside them.

"Great Spirit of the Universe," Tilly begins softly, "thank you for this bounty. We bring our minds together as one and give thanks."

She breathes in. "For Mother Earth, who gives us what we need to live in peace. For the food plants that feed us. For water, the rivers, the lakes, the oceans, that nourish all life. For Grandmother Moon, still guiding children into the world."

Camas puts her hand on Tilly's pregnant belly. Pedro licks her fingernails.

"And for Creator, for everything she's done for us."

A pause.

"Now our minds are one," Tilly finishes.

"Thanks for the shrooms," Camas adds. "Amen."

They open their eyes and smile.

Tilly picks a morel out of the bag. "These are gorgeous!"

"We had three bags, but we left one for a grizzly. Josh dumped it out as we side-stepped away."

Tilly's eyes widen. "Thank goddess you're OK!"

"And get this...once we made it down, he proposed!"

"What?!" Tilly grabs her left hand.

Camas reaches into her pocket and pulls out a blue and white hacky sack. "He proposed with his vintage 1986 Wham-O."

"Oh, Camas!" Tilly hugs her. "That's perfect."

"It's not as cool as a baby."

"Silly, of course it is. Pass the bag."

They stand and pass the footbag back and forth with practiced feet. Pedro dances between them, trying to intercept. Below, rowers slide long skulls from the boathouse onto the sparkling lake with laughter floating above.

CHAPTER 4

Hereford-Angus "Tank" – Born 80.2 lbs. Slaughtered at 18 months, 1,152 lbs. - Hot carcass weight 720 lbs.

(NATURAL LIFESPAN 20 YEARS)

Ny Greene, a compact man in his late 60s with a puff of white hair, pedals his Dutch bike up a tree-lined trail. A round cardboard tube bounces lightly on a narrow rear rack, secured by two small bungee cords. He crests a knoll into a sunlit clearing, where a tractor stirs up dust across a bare patch of ground surrounded by white oak, bur oak, red oak, and shagbark hickory.

Ny, founder of the Sereneway Agrihood, parks his bike and grabs the cardboard tube. He waves to Paignton, his farm manager, and unrolls architectural drawings on a large table overlooking tidy rows of vegetable beds and young fruit trees.

Paignton cuts the tractor engine and walks over, dust on his worn Blundstones and Carhartt overall shorts. His Des Moines rugby club shirt is streaked with sweat.

Another bicycle appears in the distance. Luxey Aster, a sprightly woman in her early 30s with a sharp brunette bob, coasts up on her city cruiser in a sun-yellow skirt, denim shirt tied at the waist, and lemon-yellow designer sneakers. She lifts a picnic basket from her bike and lays out cheese, charcuterie, tomatoes, sugar snap peas, and freestone peaches with flair. Her brightly painted fingernails flash as she slices fresh-baked bread.

Ny scans the plans, then points towards the graded soil. "The view from Polk Ridge is better than I expected."

"This is so exciting!" Luxey claps. "When do the houses pop up?! My phone won't stop ringing!"

"I thought I was prepping this site for more farmland," Paignton says, biting into a peach. "I already ordered a quarter ton of mycor-rhizal inoculum."

"What's that?" Luxey asks.

"Fungi," Ny answers.

"I did shrooms once," she muses. "I thought my gel nails were goldfish swimming." She looks at her fingernails. "They were the big goldfish. You know, like the ones in Hawaii."

"Koi," Ny says dryly, looking at the plan. He measures, then sketches boxes into the development section of the plan.

Paignton leans over the plan, chewing. "Could we work in a bigger garden? I signed on for an agri-neighborhood. So far, I see eccentric Dina shouting at people in the rows and a handful of kids planting beans. That's it."

"We offer classes, chef nights, music in the fields," Ny replies. "But turnout's low."

"Then make it mandatory," Paignton suggests. "Put it in the CC&Rs: every homeowner must work a few hours on the land."

"Oh God no," Luxey gasps. "I could never sell that. My buyers want to bike past the farm, not farm the farm."

"Maybe then they'd stop calling me to rescue them from garter snakes. And kids? What about the next generation?"

"Kids don't sign checks," Luxey shrugs, tweezering a piece of salami with her nails, popping it in her mouth.

"I'm thinking denser," Ny says. "One wastewater pond, some native grass, maybe lilies. Simple."

"Easy to please," Paignton mutters. "Just toss in a selfie arbor on a bridge by a sewer pond."

"Oh yes!" Luxey beams. "They'd love that! And, the board's pulling the farm from the website."

Ny stiffens.

"What?" Paignton coughs mid-baguette. He clears his throat. "We're still here. Supplying the restaurant and two others in town."

"They're rebranding it as 'gardens,'" Ny says with reluctant finger quotes. "More housing, same charm."

Paignton frowns, pockets a peach, and turns back to the tractor.

"Come to the Slow Earth Food Festival," Ny offers. "Take a break."

"To find a new job?"

"Hopefully not. Just some fresh air."

"Can I come too?" Luxey chirps.

"It's for farmers and philosophers."

"I read Garden and Gun."

"You'll have to drive yourself. Bring the brochures with the farm still in them. Might be some dreamer-farmers there."

"I thought we were nixing it." Luxey looks puzzled.

"We're still growing a few things," Ny mutters, redrawing lot lines.

"How many?" Luxey's eyebrows raise.

"How many what?" Paignton calls over his shoulder.

"Houses, silly."

A rust-breasted robin lands on the table, snatches a bread crust, and flies off as the tractor roars back to life. Luxey ducks.

CHAPTER 5

Blue Coco Climbing French Bean

(ENDANGERED)

Peter Cowscreek, a sun-leathered farmer in his mid-50s, walks into the Caloose County Farm Bureau in northeast Iowa. He wears faded Levi's, a blue work shirt, and beat-up leather boots dusted with the fields of Decorum. When he was five, his Dutch grandfather let him drive a tractor down Main Street, his feet barely brushing the clutch. Now, dust rests on the high ridges under his eyes, shading the white valleys of his crow's feet.

"Hey, Peter, how's it goin'?" asks Christy, the heavy-set receptionist with bold blonde highlights.

"The sun rose this morning."

"That's somethin'."

"Got coffee?"

"Yeah. Help yourself. Tony's expecting you."

Peter pours himself a cup from the old drip machine into a John Deere mug and heads toward the back office. A vintage 1900s map of Caloose County hangs on the wall.

Tony, a stocky man in a short-sleeve shirt and Lee jeans, looks up from his laptop. "How's the ranch, Pete?"

Peter sits. "Damn it all, Tony. Not so good."

"What is it this time?"

"Just when you think farming can't get any tougher."

"Shoot."

"You know I went organic in 2010."

"Yup. Caused quite a stir."

"Had to do it. It was the only way I could stay afloat without suckin' off Uncle Sam. Now I'm growin' more and I'm in the black."

"You should speak at one of our meetings."

"I'd get shot."

Tony chuckles. "Probably. But it's been nearly a hundred years since the Soil Conservation Act, and we're still leavin' bare soil to blow like L.A. smog every fall."

"Yep."

"I read we've lost 56 billion metric tons of topsoil in the Midwest due to tillage and naked fields."

"You're preachin' to the choir."

Tony leans in. "When I show farmers the research, they say, 'Everything I'm doing – pesticides, GMOs – all of it, I was told to do. I've been rewarded for it. Now I'm the bad guy?'"

Peter nods. "I hear it, too."

"They yell, 'It's not my fault! The government pushed me here!'"

"Hey, can we talk about my problems today, not just the apocalypse?" Peter says good-naturedly.

Tony laughs. "Sure thing."

"A new Baesamen rep came by yesterday. Young, slick. Gave me a pile of B.S. as tall as 801 Grand about how his seed would save my farm. No bugs, no weeds within five hundred miles."

Tony grimaces. Takes a sip of coffee.

"I told him I'm in bed with bugs and weeds. Said I'd go toe to toe with any of his customers on net returns. Alfalfa, corn, soybeans, winter wheat, walnuts. Hell, even tomatoes!"

"What'd he say?"

"That he didn't lose sleep over the weather."

"Cold."

"That science feeds the world, and it will obliterate my problems or some such bullshit."

Tony signs. That's their pitch. 'Obviator science.'

"I told him that's a damn prison. Same handcuffs whether you're in Iowa or India. And once you install a drip fertigation system, it's not your farm anymore. It's theirs."

Tony nods. "He threatened you?"

Peter stiffens. "He said if I didn't buy, I'd be sorry."

"What does that mean?"

"I don't know. Just keep your ears open, will ya?"

"Will do. I'll ask if any of the other boys have had threats."

Peter pauses. "Maybe we should cool it with the 'boys.' My niece and wife both farm."

Tony grins. "Fair point. This *wetback* understands."

Peter laughs. "Thanks, buddy."

As he walks out, a tall, young man walks in. He wears a crisp blue-checkered shirt tucked into dark Levi's, a high-brim cap, and a stoic expression.

Peter extends his hand. "Son," he says gruffly.

"Dad." They shake.

"Charlie!" Tony beams. "Congratulations on the degree. Any job bites?"

Charlie glances at Peter. "I've started at Baesamen. Seed and fertilizer sales."

Peter walks out without a word.

In a sterile white lab, Joss stands at a stainless-steel table in a lab coat, her face calm and focused. Sixteen trays of blueberries sit in front of her, labeled by source -- store, farm, brand name, and package size. She runs a spectrometer on a berry, then logs the data into her laptop. Other techs work nearby, one with romaine, one with Fuji apples.

At the Midway Café in downtown Decorum, a half-dozen farmers sit around two tables sipping coffee. A gray-haired man with thick-framed glasses and a limp shuffles across the linoleum and groans as he lowers himself into a chair. A server fills his mug.

He coughs into a blue bandana, then shoves it in his pocket. "Damn, Pete. I thought you'd died."

"Still here, Jester."

"Well, your fields say otherwise. Hit 'em with the Giddy-Up, for Christ's sake!"

"You know I gave that Agent Orange up twelve years ago."

"Well, your west-end orchard's a damn weed museum."

"It's cover crop."

"Cover crop my shriveled ass."

CHAPTER 6

Walla Walla Sweet Onion

(ENDANGERED)

Camas sits cross-legged on the deck of the One More Year offices. Paddleboarders and sailboats glide across the glimmering lake below. She is dressed in a white tunic, tights, and a scarf wrapped around her red-blonde curls, arms raised at ninety degrees, palms to the sky. Her breath pulses in rapid bursts. Pedro trots onto the deck and licks her cheek. She doesn't break her breathing rhythm.

Tilly steps out. "Hey, yogini. How are you holding up?"

"I'm offering up my limitations to my greatness." Camas opens her eyes.

"Cool. But how are you really doing?"

"I'm okay."

"You didn't talk about your mom much. I didn't realize she was so sick."

"She didn't share much with me either. She was always on the go."

Pedro curls up in Camas's lap. She strokes his head.

"You're very guru-goddess today," Tilly says. "What's with the turban?"

"A white head covering focuses energy at the third eye and symbolizes devotion," Camas says with playful pomp.

"Says who?"

"My guru in pixels. I did some long akals to help her spirit travel."

"That's beautiful. The turban's cute."

Camas pops up, dumping Pedro, and hurries inside to check her reflection. "I am pretty cute," she says, adjusting her headscarf. She spins, eyes closed.

"Don't let us interrupt, whirling dervish," Tilly says, settling at her desk.

"No, it's fine!" Camas calls. She stops, dizzy, then strips the tunic and scarf, revealing a snug black dress. She reaches into a desk drawer, pulls out a pair of black strappy sandals, and pulls them over bright red toenails.

"Where are you going?"

"Nowhere. I'm in mourning, but it still needs to be sexy."

"It's OK to be sad, you know."

"Maybe later." Camas grabs a flask and takes a long swig.

"Yoga and Jäger?" Tilly asks, puzzled.

"Balance."

"Iowa's next?"

Camas nods. "Need to pick up Mom's ashes in Decorum, plan a memorial, figure out what to do with the house. Will you come?"

"Of course."

"Thanks, sista."

"How did your mom die?"

"Cancer. She told me she had it beat."

Tilly is quiet. She breaks the silence. "Max called today. Said he's planning a food conference."

"Max! How is he?"

"He's good. Sends his condolences. He wants us to MC the Slow Mother Food festival, or something like that."

"Slow Mo Fo?"

Tilly looks at her phone. "Here it is. Slow Earth Food Festival in Dubuque, Iowa. He wants us to be Mistresses of Ceremonies. Me for intros. You for vibes."

"We'd be amazing."

"You sure you're up for it?"

"I could use the distraction." She drinks again.

Tilly lifts an eyebrow.

"And it's Jack Daniels, not Jäger."

"Since when are you day drinking?"

Camas shrugs.

"We could learn more about food injustice," Tilly offers. "Iowa's the second biggest breadbasket after California."

Camas scrolls. "Hey, the festival's less than 100 miles from the Yellow River Loop trail. Want to go bikepacking before?"

"Could be fun. Make it your bachelorette party?" Tilly asks.

"No stripper?"

"Maybe a skinny dipper."

They laugh.

"Liam's not going to let you single-track pregnant, Till."

"It's farmland. No jumps or berms. We're technically working."

Camas reads aloud, "Zero singletrack, 4,165 elevation, 90 miles round trip. Perfect for beginners, experts, even pregnant riders."

"It doesn't say that."

"But it could."

"What about skinny dipping?"

They laugh again.

Tilly and Liam swim along the shoreline, the Selkirk range towering beyond. Liam, Tilly's husband, is an athletic young man with short curly hair and sparkling blue eyes. They pause, kiss, then breaststroke toward land as Tilly talks rapidly.

Tilly steps out, water streaming over her growing belly. She picks up her towel.

Liam emerges behind her, catching up with strong, splashing strides. "You're doing what?!"

Roundup Ready™ Sugar Beet

(GMO - Monsanto)

A man in his 50s with a shiny bald head and wire-rimmed glasses stands at the window of a sleek, high-rise office. Mounted trophy animals and antique elephant tusks line the room: bear, leopard, antelope, lion. A leather speed bag hangs in the corner. Bruno Die Weise, lean in a starched white shirt, stares at a digital map of U. S. farmlands glowing across a screen. The sun sets behind him over downtown St. Louis as a motorized shade lowers.

Cleo, six feet four inches, in their 30s, strides in with a tray of black coffee and a deep red digestif. They wear a black checkered knit wrap dress and striped Psudo vegan court shoes.

"After-dinner tray, sir," Cleo says, setting it down with long, graceful fingers. "It's too damn dark in here," Cleo admonishes with a slight drawl.

"Decaf?" Bruno grunts.

"Always."

Bruno sips, then flips his phone toward Cleo. "Tell Randy I want one of our people speaking at this hippie food thing." His mild German accent floats over the liqueur.

Cleo turns on a lamp, studies the phone. "It's a slow food show."

"Slow?" Bruno snorts. "Who wants slow food?!"

"Apparently, a few thousand people."

Bruno starts pacing. "How are we supposed to top last quarter if these idiots can't sell to every farmer?"

"I don't know."

"You don't know?! I want a Baesamen speaker at that festival!"

Cleo raises an eyebrow. "It's regenerative ag."

"So?" Bruno swallows the blood-red Killepitsch in one gulp.

"We don't have anything to sell them."

"We're regenerative."

"That's...generous. You generate, sure. But there's no 're.'"

Bruno frowns. "They all need money. Maybe we sell them money."

"Mr. Die Weise?"

"You only call me 'Mr. Die Weise' when you're mad at me. Are you mad at me, too?"

"Who else is mad at you?"

"My wife. I forgot her birthday."

Cleo gestures to the wrapped gift still on his desk. "I set that there yesterday."

Bruno picks it up and hands it to them. "Put this in my car. And call Randy."

Cleo nods. "It's 7:15. Anything else before I go?"

Bruno shuffles files on his desk. "Nope... Wait. What's with those clown shoes?"

"I'm headed for a pick-up game at Forest Park."

"I thought they got rid of those courts."

"They're Black."

Bruno looks up.

"They're back," Cleo replies and walks out.

Bruno sits. He opens a file marked Carbon.

Charlie sits on the front porch, a black lab curled at his feet. He answers a call.

"Hey, Randy."

He listens.

"It's going well. Thanks."

Listens.

"No, I haven't spoken at a conference before."

Listens.

"Sure. I know the motto. Selling obviator science. SOS."

Listens.

"Got it. Send me the talking points."

Listens.

"Wait. What am I speaking about if I can't talk about the products?"

Listens.

"Right. I'll study that and give it my best."

Josh, Camas's fiancé, a young Black man with a short-trimmed beard, refills glasses from a Matchlove growler of Farmhouse Saison. The lakeside table outside Tilly and Liam's cottage glows in the sunset. They are surrounded by a feast of cream of morel soup, grilled vegetables, garden tomatoes, lemon-crema fried morels, freshly baked bread, hummus, sautéed greens, French beans with cashew-cheese herbed dipping sauce, ratatouille, morel and asparagus flatbread, and huckleberry tarts with cashew crème fraiche.

Camas strolls out of the cottage with tequila and three shot glasses. Liam passes, raising his hand, and squeezes Tilly's hand under the table. She sips sparkling water and lifts a fuchsia-purple slice of Blue Pear tomato to her mouth, closing her eyes in a silent vow of earth love.

Camas and Josh clink glasses and kiss. Tilly kisses Liam. Pedro lies beneath the table as the friends laugh under the rising moonlight, candles flickering against the lake.

CHAPTER 8

Cobb500™ Co Chicken "Snowball" – Born .09 lbs. Slaughtered at 18 weeks, 7.5 lbs. – Hot carcass weight 5.7 lbs.

(NATURAL LIFESPAN 8 YEARS)

"You can't bring that second bag," Tilly says.

"Huh?" Camas continues pulling her luggage out of the back of Josh's 1994 Subaru Sambar. It's early morning, moonlight spilling over the Sandglass train station parking lot.

"You heard me. Our bikes count as carry-ons."

Liam and Josh pull bikes and panniers from the truck. Liam puts bouncing Pedro on a leash.

"One, two," Camas says, pointing at her bike and bag. "It's a backpack."

"And your panniers," Tilly adds.

"I didn't think you'd notice since we're sneaking off like turn-of-the-last-century railroad spinsters. My cute outfits are in there, and some adult beverages."

"You don't need outfits to be cute," Josh says.

"Thank you, honey." Camas kisses Josh, then glances back at Tilly. "It's my bachelorette party. I've got stuff."

"If we were flying, we'd double our carbon footprint."

"Every lady on a train voyage deserves proper attire."

Tilly groans. "Fine. We'll pay for an extra bag. Questioning the 'lady' part."

Josh shakes his head. "I can't believe we're letting you two run off again."

"You're not supposed to see the bride before the wedding." Camas hugs him.

"That's the night before. Not weeks before."

"Liam is training on the lake with Graeme, and you said you'd enjoy time in your studio."

"I did say that. Maybe I'm rethinking."

Camas kisses him again.

"I'll keep a close eye on the application," Josh whispers.

"Thank you. I love you."

"I left the itinerary on the kitchen table, and emailed it," Tilly tells Liam.

"Remind me?" he asks.

"A day and a half on the train to La Crosse. Then we'll bike 50 miles along the Mississippi to Yellow River State Park, then south to Dubuque for the festival."

"I'm with Josh. Can I change my mind?" Liam teases.

Pedro barks.

Tilly kisses Liam, then Pedro. Camas climbs into the train. Pedro barks again. He jumps up to give her another lick. Tilly steps up onto the train.

"No, P. We're staying here," Liam says as the train pulls away.

Camas plops into a seat, pours a shot, and downs it. She looks out the window. Liam and Josh wave. Pedro barks.

CHAPTER 9

Loos Tennis Ball Lettuce

(ENDANGERED)

A smooth, strong voice sings over a crowd. A city block of row houses, each in a shade of peeling paint, stands before the plumes of gas and towering tanks of an agricultural chemical plant in the distance. Protesters hold signs in front of a chain-link fence marked with a Baesamen logo. A Black woman in her 70s stands on a wooden box, microphone in hand. The crowd sings along.

Woah, ah, mercy, mercy me
Ah, things ain't what they used to be
Where did all the blue skies go?
Poison is the wind that blows
From the north and south and east
Woah mercy, mercy me, yeah
Ah, things ain't what they used to be
Giddy-Up sprayed on the soil and in the air

Cancer-killing food everywhere

The song fades, and the matriarch leads the group to chant, "No more pesticides! Save our food! No more herbicides! Save our food! No more genocide! Save our food!"

Charlie drives down a dirt country road in his shiny new pickup truck, one elbow resting out the window. Tall corn crowds either side. Marvin Gaye's *Mercy Mercy Me* plays from the stereo.

"Protesters are gathered in front of the Baesamen plant," a TV news anchorwoman reports. "They oppose the plant's one-billion-dollar expansion. With us now is the father of environmental justice, Robert J. Bullard."

Robert Bullard appears on a split screen. Protesters chant in the background: "Hey hey ho ho! Giddy-Up has gotta go! "Hey hey ho ho! Giddy-Up has gotta go!"

"Thank you for joining us, Robert. You recently published an important article on the disproportionate environmental harm pesticides pose to people of color. Is that relevant here?"

"Absolutely, Maggie. These protesters are demanding change to a longstanding double standard in pesticides that endangers disadvantaged communities and agricultural workers worldwide."

"What can our viewers do?"

"This is not simply a pesticide issue. It's about public health and civil rights. First, find out which agency regulates pesticides in your state. In Texas, for example, it's the Department of Agriculture. Ask how to report pesticide misuse and how to receive public hearing notices. Stay informed."

"Thank you, Robert."

"You're welcome. You can connect with your local farmworkers' organization, sometimes a union, sometimes a nonprofit, and become an ally. These protesters are fighting for the health of all people, regardless of income or race."

The chant swells, "Wrong complexion. No protection!"

Tilly talks on her phone across from Camas in the restaurant car on the train.

"That was Olivier Clan. He heard we're headed to the food festival and said one of his students wants to interview us."

"About what?"

"The speakers, I think. Something about tobacco."

"Wait... tobacco? At a food festival?"

Tilly shrugs. "Olivier always has a twist. Are you working on your jokes for the festival?" Tilly asks.

"Yep. What do you call a cow with no legs?"

"I don't know."

"Ground beef."

"Maybe skip the dead cow jokes?"

"OK. What do you call a cow with no calf?"

"Sad?"

"Decaffeinated."

"Aww."

"How about, 'What did the farmer say when he lost one of his cows?'"

"Here, Bessy?"

"What a miss-steak... Mistake. Miss-steak."

Tilly frowns. "Camas, imagine cows laughing at a farmer getting trapped under a tractor. They wouldn't."

"Fair. Try this. What did the girl mushroom say to the boy mushroom?"

"I give up."

"You're a fungi."

Tilly stays serious.

"Fun guy. Fungi. Get it?"

"I got it. It's better. Keep working, sista."

"Tough audience. How are you prepping?"

"I'm working on story intros. They say stories can shift a cultural narrative."

"Like?"

Tilly reads from her laptop. "Four years ago, in California's Central Valley, a woman named Rogelina was pruning vines with co-workers when she started choking. Her head pounded, her mouth turned bitter, and she began vomiting. So did others. A cloud of pesticide had drifted in from a nearby orchard. Fifty-two people were affected. Six went to the hospital. One was kept overnight. And that's just the immediate damage."

"Damn. I think we'll need more jokes."

CHAPTER 10

Daubenton Kale

(ENDANGERED)

Tilly and Camas cycle from La Crosse, Wisconsin, south along the Mississippi River, along paved and gravel roads with green forests mixed with small farms. Loaded panniers hang over their mountain bikes' front and back wheels. An action camera is strapped on Camas's helmet.

"Death by 1,000 hills," Camas pants, straining uphill.

"That guy in the pub wasn't kidding."

"You're not even winded."

"A little. Quit complaining," Tilly says.

"Sat nam. Sat nam. Sat nam," Camas chants through her breath.

"What's that?"

"A mantra. I'm calling on my yogi mind powers. Sat nam. Sat nam. Pils-ner. Pils-ner. Pils-ner."

Tilly shakes her head.

They reach the hilltop and unclip from their pedals. Standing over their bikes, they gaze out across a lush sweep of sugar maple, white ash, red elm, and hickory trees.

"See? Worth it?" Tilly asks, sipping from her Refill Bill water bottle. The pug mascot, Plastic, beams in a superhero cape. "I see emerald green, celadon green, forest..."

"Money green," Camas cuts in. "Mint chip ice cream green."

"No looking at your phone, cheater."

"I'm not. I'm taking a photo. Smile!" She snaps one of Tilly. "Tequila lime green!"

"Come here. Let's take one together."

Camas leans her bike against a tree, joins Tilly, and throws an arm around her best friend. They grin at the camera. Camas unzips her pannier and pulls out a beer.

"Seriously?"

"Four miles to camp. I earned it," she says, cracking it open.

They push off again, taking a couple of hops to get their loaded bikes moving.

"Chartreuse!" Camas yells.

"Alfalfa."

"Neon green."

"Teal."

"John Deere green!"

"That's not a real color," Tilly says.

"Is too. And a country song."

"Jade."

"Midori!"

"Emerald."

"Al Green."

They ride on, laughing.

Camas stirs a pot on a campfire under the trees. Her middle finger, wrapped in gauze, sticks out defiantly. The bikes are locked to a picnic table beside their tents.

She ladles black beans into bowls, adds cashew mozzarella, and hands one to Tilly. She sits beside her, eating from the pot. She opens warm tortillas in foil and hands one to Tilly.

"How's the finger?" Tilly asks.

"It hurts. I took that last downhill like a pro. That tree root caught my tire," Camas says, showing her skinned knee. "The helmet cam caught the whole thing."

"Maybe easy on the beer tomorrow. Anyway, I had a thought as we rode."

"Shoot."

"You know the preppers in Sandglass?"

"You mean the preppers everywhere?"

"Yeah. I don't know much about them, but I know they worry about the end of the world. And I know most of them have guns...and some of those guns are killing people. But that's not what this is about."

"Then what?" Camas takes a swig.

"They stockpile, right? They teach survival skills, preparing for some cataclysmic event."

"SHTF."

"What?"

"They're preparing for when the shit hits the fan," Camas says with food in her mouth.

"SHTF, OK. But what if they could help the slow food movement? They believe in individual, small-scale food production. What if we met them where they are?"

"Say more."

"Let's pretend that you and Josh think the world is coming to an end and that we need to build a wall because a person of color is coming to take your job."

"Josh is Black. Not sure this fits."

"Just pretend. And you don't want to have anything to do with a tofu-eating woman of color like me, but you think climate change will kill us before the racial apocalypse, so he's in."

"OK."

"You've got three little unvaccinated kids – hungry, growing, adorable."

"I like kids," she says wistfully. "Mine will believe in science."

"Sure. You open YouTube, and there's a step-by-step guide to soil prep, seed saving, and composting. You start growing enough food to feed the neighborhood. You barter, you teach others."

"We start our own channel! What am I growing?" Camas asks.

"Everything. Rest assured, not GMO corn."

"What do we call it?"

"C&J Acres? Guru Goddess Greens?"

"Patanjali Peaches?!" Camas says in a slow southern drawl. "I can build back better with my Make America Great Again victory garden!"

"Yes! And soon your neighbors are baking with your peaches, you're trading pizza crust for greens, and suddenly you're not self-sufficient, you're community sufficient."

"I like it better than hiding in a bunker with powdered cheese."

"Right? To green dreams and radical neighbors," Tilly raises her aluminum bottle.

Camas clinks it with her beer.

CHAPTER 11

Artic™ "Golden Delicious" Apple

(GMO – OKANAGAN SPECIALTY FRUITS INC.)

"This is it," Camas says, turning onto a dirt road lined with rows of lush peach trees under a clear blue sky. She stops, leans her bike against a tree, and takes a drink from her water bottle.

"Peaches!" Tilly says, smiling.

"The ranch is about 800 acres...peaches, almonds, walnuts, pistachios, fruit trees, and row crops."

"That sunflower field we passed was stunning."

"I used to run through them when I was little."

"I can picture you. A little toe head with dirt on her knees," Tilly teases.

Camas laughs. "The house is this way."

They walk their bikes down the dusty lane.

"That was right before my parents divorced, and I had to move to Sandglass with my dad."

"Too bad about the divorce, but lucky for me," Tilly says. "You own 800 acres?"

"No, just this house and about 30 acres. When my dad found out I was dating Josh, he wrote me out of the will. The only reason I got this house is that my mother got it in the divorce. My dad and stepmom weren't too excited about having a Black grandchild."

"That's messed up."

"Yep, but I'd rather have Josh than a bunch of dirt."

They walk in silence.

"Remember when my stepmom used to drop me off at kindergarten?" Camas asks.

"Yeah."

"I used to tell her what I was going to be when I grew up, the jumps I'd take on skis, the cabins and forts I'd build with you. Once I told her how big my boobs were going to be." Camas glances down and shrugs.

"That sounds like you."

"She used to tell me that I had 'delusions of grandeur' and needed to knock it off."

"I'm sorry."

"Luckily, I didn't know what that meant back then. I thought she was saying 'cushions of manure.' Pillows of shit might have been better than being told to stop dreaming."

Tilly shakes her head. "My people don't have that phrase."

"Really?"

"We believe that feeling of greatness comes from the spirit within. Grandeur isn't delusional, it's sacred. It means we're aligned with the Great Spirit."

Camas nods, absorbing it. "So, I wasn't having delusions of grandeur. I am grandeur."

"Yes, you are."

"Randy called," Cleo says over speakerphone. "He found a speaker for the Slow Earth Food Festival, one of our seed and chemical guys in Iowa. Just finished the training program."

Bruno scowls. "Sounds too green."

"He's hyped. Randy said he's ready to roll after the Baesamen indoctrination."

"Cleo, seriously? Indoctrination? Don't use that word outside this office."

"I usually say they are 'inculcated with ideas, attitudes, cognitive strategies, and methodologies.'"

Bruno smirks. "That's better. Most Americans wouldn't know what inculcated means."

"Bottom line: he's drunk the Kool-Aid."

"He better bring in business from that woke, grass-grazing, lesbitarian vegilantes conference."

Cleo raises an eyebrow. "How did it become a lesbian food show? And do you even know what woke means?"

"Just that Trump says it a lot."

"It comes from Black culture. It just means being politically aware. Awake...'woke'."

"Well, I like Trump's meaning better. Let's keep the woke from waking up anybody else."

Cleo starts fake static on the line. "I'm losing you, boss. Bad connection...kkkkhhhhkkkk." They hang up. "Woke out."

Cleo taps their phone. "Hey, Dubs. Call the guys. I need a game tomorrow."

Pause.

"Yeah, I'm stressed. I've got to get the hell out of this poison prison."

Tilly reaches up to pick a peach.

"Stop!"

"I can't even have a peach?"

"This farm isn't organic. God knows what's sprayed on there."

Tilly sighs, setting the peach gently on the ground. "Hard to believe something that beautiful could be toxic."

They reach the white farmhouse with its weathered front porch, surrounded by heirloom and prairie roses in faded shades of pink and red, and tall White Oaks.

"Wow, Cam. What a cool place!"

They leave their bikes and head upstairs, a few creaky floorboards echoing behind them. Camas opens the door to a little girl's room. Shelves lined with Rescue Heroes flank a twin bed covered with a handmade quilt.

"Aww, this was your room," Tilly whispers.

A tiny desk with cupholders for crayons sits in the corner. Above it, drawings of Pokémon figures fill the wall, fastened by crooked, aged tape pieces.

"Nice drawings. That one looks like a turkey vulture."

"That's Manibuzz. And that's Vullaby, her baby form."

"This one looks like you." Tilly points to a pink, round-faced Poké-mon with a spiked blond bob.

"That's Smoochum. You know I like smooching Josh."

"You sure do."

Proudly, Camas continues, "These are all the female Pokémon. Alcremie, Blissey, Bounsweet, Chansey…"

Tilly interrupts, "You've got drawing skills, sista. And it's sweet your mom kept all this."

"She really wanted a grandchild," Camas says quietly.

Tilly turns toward a corner covered in goddess statues: Virgin Marys, Virgen de Guadalupe, Guanyin, Shakti, and other goddess figurines of various sizes, colors, and shapes, all holding a peaceful, silent court on a hot pink faux-fur rug atop a chest.

"Whoa. Are these your virgin mother Pokémon? I didn't realize you were such a fan of Mary?"

Camas laughs. "You've seen the tattoo." Camas points to your tattoo sleeve.

"Yes, but there must be thirty of them."

"My dad yelled a lot. At Mom. At me. I'd lie in my bed and talk to Mary. Mom taught me to meditate. I'd put one of these statues in my pocket and go for a long walk."

"Why didn't you tell me?"

"Your spirits make more sense to me now. They're part of nature. Mine were about surviving."

"I can see the appeal. I bet Mary liked nature, too." Tilly stands in front of the statues. One...tall, with flowing hair, resembles her. "I meant, why didn't you tell me about the abuse?"

Camas shrugs. "Whining sucks. There weren't beatings. Just stuff like calling my mom a n****r lover because she was liberal, showing up drunk at my school, or throwing the tuna casserole on the sidewalk. Shit like that."

"Why'd he do that?"

"Who the fuck knows. Probably because he was drunk and hated tuna casserole." Her voice cracks.

"I'm sorry." Tilly hugs her.

"Thanks." Camas turns to the window. She wipes an eye.

"Are you OK?"

"I miss Mom."

"Are you going to keep this place?" Tilly asks.

"I don't know yet."

They sit silently.

Camas stands, stretching. "Hey, let's see if there's any grub in the pantry."

As they reach the door, Camas stops. She picks up a five-inch-tall Mary statue from the pink fur altar and slips it into Tilly's pocket.

Tilly smiles.

As Camas reaches for her hoodie on the back of the chair, a hot-pink envelope catches her eye from underneath a vase on the dresser.

She picks it up, staring at the looping handwriting spelling Camas Lily on the front.

"What's that?" Tilly asks.

"It's my mom's handwriting," Camas says quietly. "It's a letter to me."

She tucks it into her sweatshirt pocket. "I'll read it later."

Want to read the letter Camas found? Download the free short story "Dear Camas Lily" (with a peach shortcake recipe) at aviskalfsbeek.co m/camaslily.

CHAPTER 12

American Bison "Thunderhoof" – Born 48 lbs. Slaughtered at 18 months, 785 lbs. - Hot carcass weight 471 lbs.

(NATURAL LIFESPAN 20 YEARS)

A bee buzzes through a montage of mono-mutated fields, meat mortuaries, maverick farmers, and magical maples. The soft harmonies of "Pachamama" by Beautiful Chorus float through the breeze.

A colorful collection of pastel bee houses rests in a meadow of wild-flowers with rolling hills in the distance. A scattering of black and white Holstein cows graze in the long grass. A bee lands on a calf's nose.

A hawk glides above an endless sweep of cornfields. It circles down to an oak tree near a small apple orchard. A woman steps out of her truck, pulls on her beekeeper hood and gloves, and walks to a line of wooden hives. She lifts the lid on one, peers inside, and solemnly cups her hands around a pile of dead bees.

The morning sun casts a golden light on a small, thriving farm. Rows of colorful lettuce, squash, peppers, garlic, artichokes, eggplant, and corn glow in the early warmth. Fruit trees and borders of sunflowers, sweet peas, zinnias, peonies, roses, and juvenile eucalyptus encircle a centerpiece of multicolored heirloom tomatoes.

Dewdrops catch the light on clusters of dark purple, orange, yellow, green, and red tomatoes hanging heavy from staked bushes. Under an overhang beside a weathered red barn, Carmella, a young artist-farmer, wears a tank top reading *Mi Cuerpo – Yo Decido* and denim-patched overalls embroidered with a bouquet. She carefully arranges tomatoes from a wicker basket onto an old wooden table.

Starting at the bottom, she builds a living rainbow heart: deep eggplant, striped, red-green, firm green tomatoes, artichokes widening the base. Then comes the sunny yellows, bright oranges, and finally the red tomatoes and crimson bells at the top. She adds flower blossoms, zinnias, marigolds, cosmos, tucked into their matching color rows.

A fluffy Buff Orpington chicken hops onto the table just as Carmella places the final tomato. She picks the chicken up, kisses her head, then lifts her phone and snaps a photo of her vibrant, edible artwork.

A Black Angus cow shuffles forward into a narrow chute, hemmed in by steel bars. The squeeze cage locks around him. A man raises a wood-handled pistol and fires a rod into the cow's forehead. The animal collapses, neck limp, eyes dulled, mouth ajar. In the holding area behind, another cow lets out a low, mournful cry. The serpentine-curved chute hides nothing.

Dangling yellow-green flower stalks drape from sugar maples at an organic syrup farm in Garnavillo, Iowa. Bees flit between blossoms. A breeze carries pollen in slow, sacred arcs, co-conspirators in the trees' sweet rituals.

Two men in dusty Levi's and work shirts lean against a pickup at the edge of a freshly tilled field. A German Shorthaired Pointer puppy bounds out of the cab and spins circles in the soft dirt, kicking up a cloud of powder. One farmer lifts his bandana to cover his mouth. The other grabs the pup and hoists it into the truck bed, then dumps water from a cooler over the pup's back. The dog shakes. The man dries it with a towel, scrubs his own hands with soap and water, throws the dog into the cab, and climbs in.

A tillage trailer pulled by Belgian draft horses breaks soil past rows of Komastuna mustard greens, Blue Scotch kale, Verdil spinach, and Red Romaine lettuce. A mother and toddler walk between rows of heirloom tomatoes and melons. She clips wild fennel and lemon basil, then tucks them into a basket. The boy flaps his arms in glee when the horses pass.

A Latina woman stands at the edge of a field holding a clipboard and speaking to a group of female farm workers. They wear boots, scarves over their faces, and wide-brimmed hats. A young man drives a tractor in the next field, pulling a 90-foot boom sprayer through rows of crops. Inside the sealed, air-conditioned cab, *Mother Earth Provides for Me* by the Nitty Gritty Dirt Band plays on the radio.

AVIS KALFSBEEK

In a cityscape framed by three-story brick apartments, a Black woman in a straw hat walks through rows kale, lettuce greens, radishes, cucumbers, cherry tomatoes, and strawberries. She pauses near a trellis heavy with blackberries. A green butterfly is painted on the side of a corrugated work shed beside her. Above it, in bold hand-drawn letters: *Three Part Harmony Farm*.

CHAPTER 13

The Boothby's Blonde Cucumber

(ENDANGERED)

"The sign says Tree House," Bruno mutters into his phone, looking up from the sidewalk.

"That's right, sir," Cleo replies.

"I'm meeting Red Glatze. We're not going to be seated next to hippies with B.O., are we?"

"It's a trendy plant-based restaurant, sir. I thought it would be good for you and the Secretary of Agriculture's image to be seen dining there on Meatless Monday. You bathed today, correct?"

"Don't be a smart aleck." Bruno hangs up and walks into the restaurant, scowling.

The evening sun glows behind a tree-lined country road. Silhouettes of two cyclists crest a gentle hill. Camas and Tilly, dusty and sweat-streaked, bathed in golden light, turn into a gated property. Quaint cottages and country homes with vegetable beds line the tree-lined path. Fruit and nut orchards stretch into the distance.

They stop in front of a stately modern farmhouse beside a tall glass Victorian greenhouse. The greenhouse door bursts open.

A man with wild grey hair, like snowy egret feathers, emerges, beaming. "Welcome to Sereneway! You must be Tilly and Camas! I'm Ny Green," he calls, extending his hand.

"Hello. This place is beautiful," Tilly says, shaking his hand while straddling her bike.

"Hi. Nice digs," Camas adds with a wave.

"Thank you. We're assembling up the hill." Ny gestures toward a patio of mingling guests. "Come join us."

"We'll knock those people right off that hill if we don't shower first," Camas jokes, sniffing her armpit.

"You're fine. Cocktails have started."

"We'll be quick," Tilly says.

"Your cottage is just down this lane. Michael will lead you."

A teenage boy in a white Sereneway polo and khaki shorts hops on a cruiser bike and gestures to them to follow.

They ride past a small herd of cows and sheep. Tilly catches the gaze of a cow as they pass. "Why are we here again?" she asks.

"Max suggested it. Ny's speaking at the festival, and it's on our route."

Michael stops in front of a cottage with overflowing window boxes of rainbow chard and nasturtiums. "This is it," he says, parking his bike.

He opens their door and hands Tilly the key. "Can I bring in your..."

"Panniers," Camas interjects. "We're good." She yanks hers off and rushes in. "I'll shower first!"

"Thanks, Michael. Cool tattoo," Tilly adds. "Is that a cow hoof?"

"It's a fist and pig hoof."

"Animal rights?"

"Yep. I'm headed to a vegan campout next week. Music, speakers, and a protest at a large pig slaughterhouse in Ottumwa."

"Good for you."

Michael nods and pedals away. "Enjoy your stay."

"Thanks," Tilly says, raising a fist as he rides off.

Tilly and Camas make their way up the hill. Tilly wears a sleeveless dusty rose-colored knit dress and a gold locket. Her legs are strong from riding, her arms tan-lined. Camas wears a white sari-like tunic over white leggings with aqua flip-flops and a splint on her middle finger. Her toenails are bright pink.

Guests are seated at a long wooden table under string lights. Ny greets them and leads them to the center seats.

He raises a glass. "Friends, meet Tilly and Camas from One More Year."

The crowd applauds.

"Tilly, will you say a few words?"

Tilly stands. "Thanks for having us. This place is magical. Camas and I run One More Year. We ask people to extend the life of their things: your phone, your car, your lawn mower. If you can keep it one more year, you reduce consumption and help heal the planet. Then the next year, ask the same question."

She raises her water glass. "To keeping our stuff longer!"

The guests raise their glasses. Clinks all around.

"Nice job," Camas whispers.

"Thanks, friend. I'm beat. You?"

"Exhausted. This wine is delicious."

"Easy does it."

Servers begin circulating with platters. When a tray of red meat reaches Tilly, she gracefully raises her hand to the side of her plate. "No, thank you."

The server turns to Camas, who glances at Tilly, then at the nearby pasture, then at the blood-tinged platter. She bites her lip.

"No, thank you," Camas says quietly. "Do you have any potatoes?"

"Another glass of wine?" Camas calls from inside the cottage.

"No thanks. I didn't have a first," Tilly says from the patio chaise lounge, gazing at the stars.

Camas emerges with a bottle and her glass, sets them down, and flops beside her.

"Didn't you get enough at dinner?" Tilly asks.

Camas ignores her. They sit in silence, stargazing.

"Who do you think will be the last people to eat meat?" Camas slurs.

"Huh?"

"If there was a global ban...climate, ethics, whatever...and it was phased out, who'd be the last ones to eat it?"

"Strange question, considering you ate it yesterday."

"I didn't today, though, did I?"

"No. Thank you."

"I keep wondering what makes our minds shift. Why are horses off-limits?"

"I'm not sure."

"Remember when they found horse meat in Nestle pasta and people were freaked?"

"I remember."

"And alpacas? Too cute, I guess."

"I know why I don't eat them."

Camas's voice rises. "Why are humans off limits? There were cannibals once."

"OK, now you're really out there. Is it the wine?"

Camas lifts her wine glass. "It's in glass, not a SOLO cup. I'm good."

"I don't know what flips a switch," Tilly says. "But I do know Ireland passed the first animal cruelty law in the 1600s...no tearing wool from live sheep. Time for bed?"

"You didn't answer. Would beef become rare? The elite chasing the last cuts like they do with Kobe? A mad race for mad cows?"

Tilly nods slowly. "There would be sanctuaries. We wouldn't need to finish eating them."

"Or a race to the last steak? A free-for-all, like a Stephen King Hunger Games. A million bucks for the final bite instead of a ride to space."

"That's tragically ironic...we're rocketing to space because of beef," Tilly says.

Camas chuckles. "Picture it. An elegant engraved invite. A mansion in the hills. A table of elites slicing into the final cow."

"Camas, put that wine down. That's utterly morbid."

"You just made a cow joke. Udder-ly."

Tilly doesn't laugh.

Camas stares into her glass. "The last barbarians."

CHAPTER 14

The Colossal Leek

(ENDANGERED)

Camas and Tilly sleep in full-size beds in a white cottage with fresh flowers and high-thread-count linens. Tilly sits up and stretches. She gets out of bed. Her tan legs are sleek and strong under her nightshirt. She walks to the window and pulls open the curtain. The sun shines onto Camas's face.

"Hey! That's too bright!" Camas moans, pulling the sheet over her head.

"Rise and shine, sleepyhead. We're supposed to tour with the Marketing Director at eight."

"Didn't we see enough of Miss Butter Lettuce last night? This place seems a bit hoity-toity to be saving the world."

"Luxey's her name. I think we can save the world at all price points," Tilly says, yanking off the sheet. "Now get up. Ny said there will be peach pancakes."

There is a knock at the door.

Tilly opens it and finds a package. "What's this?"

"My potato chips!"

"You ordered potato chips?"

"We were out in the sticks burning calories, and I was craving Burt's Guinness Thick Cut."

Tilly stares at her.

"I know what you're thinking?"

"What am I thinking?"

"You're thinking: why did I spend fifty bucks on six packs of salty beer-loving spuds?"

"And?"

"You mean why I used jet fuel to get them from Devon, England?"

"They're from England?!"

"Probably from the local distribution warehouse, but still."

"How did they get there?" Tilly folds her arms.

"Maybe not on the sailboat with Greta?" Camas shrugs.

"Not funny."

"What are you doing here?" Peter says from his pickup truck.

"A son can't visit his father?"

"I'll see you Sunday. Not sure why you had to come all the way out."

"Can you get out of the truck, Dad?"

"You know how much there is to do around here?"

"I used to work here. Come on, Pete."

Peter frowns, gets out, and shuts the door. "Go on. I've got to get the guys on the next field."

"To get rid of those nasty weeds?"

"They're not nasty. They're voluntary cover crop."

"That adds up." Charlie mimes flipping cash with his thumb.

"No, not really. Input costs are down, production is up. Thinning is just a blip."

"A blip, huh?" Charlie shakes his head. "I can't come to dinner Sunday."

"You could've called."

"I'm launching a new offering at a food festival in Dubuque."

"Baesamen doesn't do offerings. Only offings."

"Just listen."

"I'm not interested."

"I need to practice my presentation. Come on. Let the weeds grow, dammit."

Peter sighs. "Alright, but I'll be critiquing, not listening."

Charlie clears his throat. "Thank you for inviting me to the Slow Earth Food Festival."

"We're here to slowly kill it," Peter mutters.

Charlie pushes on. "I'm here to announce a tremendous offer."

"Snake oil."

"You can participate in the boom of carbon credits--and you don't have to do a thing."

Peter is silent.

Charlie smiles, surprised.

"Don't mistake silence for interest. Just waiting for the other shoe to drop."

"That's right. It is exciting! We'll pay you per acre just for enrolling your land! And, there are exclusive benefits!"

Peter waits.

"You'll get education materials, kickbacks on farm equipment, and a free, sophisticated farm app called Soil Topological Universal Cash Kernel. We call it 'Kernel.'"

"You can't say kickbacks. In any case, it sounds like horse crap."

"It's free."

"Nothing's free, son. I don't want to be stuck with S.T.U.C.K. or Kernel, or whatever the hell it is."

"There's no cost to sign up."

"So, I don't have to sign anything," Peter says dryly.

"Just a little digital acknowledgment."

Peter squints. "So I do sign something."

"Well, yeah, the app tracks your farm's data, so we—I mean you — can better understand it."

"Uh huh."

"And you'll be listed in the carbon program."

"I'm a farmer. I sell crops. I don't sell my data to banker-scoundrel-eco-scammers."

Peter walks to the tomato fields, kneels, and touches a seedling.

"I need to hit my numbers, Dad. It's free. For Christ's sake."

Peter stands, quiet for a beat. "Free for someone's sake, but I doubt if it's Jesus's."

He thinks. "Put your mom's 100 acres in there, the Hageman Ranch. The floodplain parcel inside the levee. It's in safflower this year."

"Thanks, Dad!" Charlie offers his iPad. "Just sign here."

Peter swipes his finger across the screen.

Charlie wipes soil smudges with his sleeve. "I'll show you how to use it when I'm back."

"No rush. Travel safe."

Peter offers his hand. They shake. As he climbs into his old truck, Charlie nods at the front seat.

"You're still using that old aluminum lunchbox."

"One more year. Works just fine," Peter says, and drives off.

Camas stands outside a roadside mercantile with weathered red paint. Her bike leans against Tilly's on the deck. She pulls her phone off the handlebars and taps it.

"Hey sexy, how's the painting going?" Camas says cheerily.

"Hey! I miss my naked muse," Josh replies.

"I miss you, too."

"How's the trip?"

"We made a detour to McGregor, Iowa, to see the very first tractor made by a Mr. Froelich in 1892."

"That's cool."

"I didn't think it was worth the extra 25 miles, but it's surprisingly interesting. Tilly's inside using the John. Any word from the adoption agency?"

"They're still researching and interviewing people."

"Like who?"

"My parents said they called them."

"So they'll call my dad and stepmom."

"Probably."

"How can parents who weren't good parents give references?"

"Not sure. How are you?"

"I miss you."

"You already said that, but I like hearing it again. Tilly told me you hurt your finger."

"I did."

"Maybe ease up on the beer?"

"It's my bachelorette party, remember?"

"I want you to have fun, but be safe."

"I can stop anytime. Hey, how about this? I won't drink until we hear from the agency. We'll celebrate then."

"That sounds great. I love you."

Tilly walks out of the store.

"Hey lover, we're getting back on the road. Gotta go. I love you, too."

CHAPTER 15

Rainbow™, SunUP™ Payaya

(GMO – CORNELL UNIVERSITY & UNIVERSITY OF HAWAII)

Bruno sits across from Red Glatze, a man in his 60s with jet-black dyed hair and a half-inch of gray roots. He wears aviator glasses, a gray suit, and a navy tie.

"I assume this was important enough to fly me to St. Louis," Red says.

"Your secretary said you had other business here."

"She's polite like that. But your lobbying reports are public. Can't nine million buy you a lobbyist who comes to me?"

"Haven't you missed me?" Bruno grins.

Red laughs. "I'm hungry. There's that." He picks up the menu.

"What's this about California announcing a task force to eliminate pesticides by 2030?" Bruno asks.

"Yes, we're involved."

"We can't feed the world without controlling pests," Bruno says.

"Some think we don't need chemicals to do that. This slow food movement may be proving it." Red responds.

"Your predecessor, Butz, said 'food is a weapon,' didn't he? He moved men off farms and into factories with 'go big or go home.' Now you want mom and pop homesteads to save the planet?" Bruno's German accent thickens, his face reddens. "We've invested billions to bring machine intelligence to farming. Now it's AI. Big Tobacco bought us big food companies. We got addicted to factory food. And now you're letting these treehugger, pot-smoking, commune-building bums reclaim land? We need to stomp out this blip of going back to the farm!"

"There are already over three million organic farms, Bruno. It's more than a blip. And now the injun's Land Back movement extends to Blacks, rag heads, queers, and pussies," Red says with a grimace.

"BIPOC-plus," Bruno mutters, taking a bite of his sandwich.

"Land speculation kept them out. But now they're trying to take land off the market entirely."

"Commons, or some such bullshit," Bruno spits. "For Christ's sake. Get your guy on that task force. Rattle the fear cage. Get those beetles, borers, and fruit flies in 3-D like a Godzilla movie."

"Governor Handsome wants clean water. Seems most people do.," Red says flatly.

Bruno grunts. They sit in silence.

"How's the plant pork?" Red asks.

"Huh?" Bruno lifts the top bun from his sandwich. "It said pulled pork."

"Phony pig."

"Waiter!" Bruno flaps his hand in the air. "Come!"

The waiter steps over. "Yes, sir."

"What the hell is in this sandwich?"

"Would you like something else?"

"That's not what I asked. What is this stuff?" Bruno points to the dark-orange filling.

"Oyster mushrooms, jackfruit, heirloom tomato paste, homemade ketchup, brown sugar, dijon mustard..."

"Jack what?"

"Jackfruit," Red supplies.

The server continues, "...liquid smoke, and organic apple cider vinegar with The Mother."

"What mother?"

"A byproduct of yeast and bacteria," Red says, sipping his drink.

"Take this jack off away!" Bruno barks, lifting the plate.

"I'm sorry you don't care for it. May I bring something else?"

"No!"

The waiter retreats, rolling his eyes.

"You're in the food industry," Red says. "Don't you know anything about food?"

"We don't sell food. We sell science."

"That's true. Polls say people want food that doesn't kill them. The woke want it to heal them."

"Right-wing media say people want burgers. Baesamen will get control of natural processes, just like that damn vinegar mother. Just watch."

"Some say Mother Earth is in control now," Red says. "Some wonder if humans even deserve to be saved."

"Scheisse! Forget all that. How are you going to rein in the California task force? We can't let that no-pesticide crap spread. You owe me."

"Damn you, Bruno." Red sighs, staring out the window. "Maybe we limit it. Keep the door open on 'low-risk' pesticides. Throw in some fear. Will that do?"

"That door's big enough," Bruno says, tossing his napkin onto the table.

CHAPTER 16

Yorkshire Hog "Herman" — Born 2.9 lbs. Slaughtered at 7 months, 281 lbs. — Hot carcass weight 197 lbs.

(NATURAL LIFESPAN 18 YEARS)

Cleo stands next to Paul, a stocky White man in his 40s with curly hair and thick glasses strapped behind his head, at the edge of a Mondrianesque-painted basketball court.

"Team Slay-ups, pick first," says Cleo, wearing a white t-shirt that reads No blood on my plate.

"Adofo!" Paul calls.

"Hopper!" Cleo continues.

"Percy!"

"Dubois!"

The six players move to their positions. Paul tosses the ball to Percy, and the three-on-three begins. Cleo launches a jump shot from outside the key. The ball whooshes through the net. Dubois, "Dubs" for short, gives Cleo a high five. The three-on-three play resumes as loud music floats over trees to the rooftop of the Missouri History Museum.

The friends play hard, laughing at bad shots and puffing up, chests out, at the good.

After the game, Cleo drinks from a water fountain at the edge of the court. They pull a knit knee-length wrap skirt from their bag and tie it around their waist.

"Listen up, fools," Cleo calls.

"Who are you callin' fools? I think the Slay-ups cleaned the court with the Balla-arenas today," Percy says with bravado.

"I wouldn't say it was a clean-up." Hopper straightens up. "We'll see you next game."

"Listen up, champions," Cleo says again. "If we had some food gardens bordering this court, we wouldn't have to walk two miles for edible grub."

"What are you talking about? There's fast food around here," Dubs says.

"And a Whole Paycheck at the end of the park," Hopper adds.

"And they've got a whole lot of GMO foods in there these days," Adofo says. "They were just in the news… 'bioengineered' Frankenstein sweet corn."

"And the white soul food in the hood has killed as many of us as the White man has," Hopper adds.

"I could use a healthy snack right now," Paul says.

"Exactly," Cleo responds. "So could those kids over there." They nod toward teenagers on the court.

"Man, I've got enough honey-dos from the ball and chain," Adofo says.

"You'd gain points if you bring your queen some greens, you lazy thug. I'll get the supplies. You just need to stay late after play next week. How about it?"

"Damn, Cleo. Don't we have enough community gardens?" Paul asks.

"Are you there volunteering? No, you're here playing ball. You had the dagger today. Why don't you add some depth?"

"You're floppin' now, man. I go to synagogue. Central Reform."

Cleo raises their voice, "You know damn well this is your church."

"True," Paul answers.

Adofo and the others nod in agreement.

"Well then, let's garden this ghost ghetto."

"Thanks for driving," Luxey says, applying lipstick in the mirror of Paignton's 1964 blue Chevy Stepside.

"Sure thing."

She reaches for the old truck stereo.

"Oh, that's not working yet. Sorry."

"Oh, my." She looks out the window.

Paignton rolls his eyes. "We'll be there before you know it."

"Two and a half hours."

"Three in this rig."

Luxey sighs. "So tell me why you like farming."

"When people ask me that, I tell them to Google: 'Wendell Berry why do farmers farm?'"

Luxey taps on her phone. She reads aloud, "Why do farmers farm? Love. They must do it for love."

"That's it."

She continues. "Farmers farm for the love of farming. They love to watch and nurture the growth of plants. They love to live in the presence of animals. They love to work outdoors. They love the weather, maybe even when it is making them miserable. They love to live where they work and to work where they live. If the scale of their farming is small enough, they like to work in the company of their children and with the help of their children. They love the measure of independence that farm life can still provide. I have an idea that a lot of farmers have gone to a lot of trouble merely to be self-employed to live at least a part of their lives without a boss."

Luxey is quiet for a beat. "That's what he said. What do you say?"

Paignton thinks. "I like seeing something from its very start to its completion. From putting a seed in the ground to eating it."

"That does sound nice."

"It is."

"It's just so darn dirty."

CHAPTER 17

Sea Island White Flint Corn

(ENDANGERED)

Tilly and Camas walk briskly along a paved path flanked by oversized metal sculptures beside the Mississippi River. In the distance, the glass modern façade of the Dubuque Grand River Conference Center reflects the midday light. Bluegrass music pours from an enormous white mega-tent ahead, open-sided and brimming with movement. People rush with purpose, setting up booths and exhibits. Handcarts and electric golf carts zip past, loaded with potted plants, sacks of seeds, cookware, signs, artwork, digital displays, and more plants. Smokers and tabletop grills sizzle with vibrant, herb-dusted food. Exhibitors hand out samples to farmers, chefs, and dreamers.

"Max!" Tilly calls, waving toward the tent's entrance.

Maximo, rugged, charismatic, and Italian-American, mid-30s with long, silky, dark hair, turns from directing a crew. He wears a celadon green Achkan jacket, narrow white silk pants, silver bracelets, and an emerald-green headband.

"Tilly and Camas! Don't you look healthy and beautiful!" Max exclaims, hugging them both tightly.

"You're looking elegant yourself," Tilly says. "Camas has some outfits like that."

"Maybe you should change into one... after a shower," Max says, wrinkling his nose playfully.

"Sorry, man. We just rode in and barely had time to lock the bikes," Camas says.

"You're fine. Come on." Max beckons them deeper into the bustle.

"How'd you get this food gig?" Camas asks, raising her voice over a mandolin solo.

"Civic planning cred as an Elder of Burning Man. I've been pushing to transition the festival to plant-based. A couple of years ago, I walked Black Rock City after the Man burned, and noticed all these barbecues over the embers."

"They were cooking meat on the wood sculpture?" Tilly asks.

"The Man," Camas corrects.

"They were eating meat off of The Man?" Tilly frowns.

"Yep. There's always been a ton of meat at Burning Man. Not surprising. Everyone brings their food, and only about five percent of Americans are vegetarian."

"That sounds hard to shift," Camas says.

"No harder than real life," Tilly says.

"When next year's theme was announced – Animalia -- I knew I couldn't support celebrating animals in elaborate art while putting them on our forks."

"What'd you do?" Tilly asks.

"Got permission to do research. I called Portman Royal for advice. He told me about this festival. Then they asked me to help with the logistics."

"The Portman Royal?" Tilly's eyes widen.

"Yes?" comes a deep voice from behind, cutting through the strumming guitars.

Tilly turns quickly.

A tall, gray-haired man with a flowing white beard approaches, dressed in cream linen pants and shirt beneath a long, cable-knit vest. A metal tree pendant hangs from a leather cord around his neck.

"Portman, meet my friends, Tilly and Camas," Max says.

"Our MCs," Portman says warmly, his eyes kind.

"Mr. Royal, I've read all your books. One of the most important people in my life shared them with me. It's truly an honor." Tilly extends her hand.

Portman holds it in both of his. "And what is this person's name?"

"Frida. She lives in Sandglass, Idaho."

"Tell Frida hello from me."

"She'll be here. I'll introduce you."

"I'd like that very much," Portman says.

"Nice summer sweater vest," Camas says, shaking his hand.

"Thank you, I made it myself," Portman replies.

"Cool."

"Yes. Quite cool." He chuckles. "The wool came from a sheep named Duttur. Max speaks very highly of you both."

"We love Max," Camas says, punching him in the shoulder.

"Max has a noble mission. To convince one of the world's biggest parties that nine days in the desert can shift the planet's thinking. Most humans still don't consider themselves part of the animal kingdom."

"It's ironic," Max adds. "The taxonomy for animalia includes humans."

"And Portman's mission?" Tilly prompts.

"To help us live past 100," Max replies.

"Are you a hundred?!" Tilly asks, startled.

"102," Portman says simply. "We're also here to remind people to grow their own food."

"What do you mean by 'remind'?" Tilly asks.

"Governments are now turning to farmers to save us from climate catastrophe."

"Farmers, help!" Camas exaggerates.

"Yes, but they've been doing that work all along. However, after the world wars, industry needed a new outlet for wartime chemicals. It became a war on insects, plants, and soil. Families were pushed off the land – not by guns, but by policy."

"Government pushed for cheap, mass food production," Max adds. "Subsidies, crop insurance...it all encouraged scale."

"In the 70s, President Nixon's Secretary of Agriculture, Earl Butz, told farmers, 'Get big or get out,'" Portman says.

"Butz was a butt," Camas mutters.

"Today, five percent of farms produce 95 percent of our food. But when this country began, 90 percent of people were farmers."

"That's so sad," Tilly says. "Can we change that?"

"We've done it before," Portman replies. "During World War I, the Victory Gardens Campaign inspired over five million home gardens."

"What happened?" Camas asks.

"A lot," Max says. "In 1916, the first Piggly Wiggly opened in Memphis. By the '20s, supermarkets were everywhere."

"Advertising convinced people that convenience was better," Portman says solemnly. "They didn't know they were trading nutrition for ease."

"Now, we tap a phone and it shows up at the door," Camas adds.

"In Russia, over half of urban residents still keep small dacha gardens. Even with harsh winters and short seasons, they grow about half their food."

"That's hopeful," Tilly says.

"What does 'slow' mean in the Slow Earth Food Festival?" Camas asks.

Portman smiles. "A good question."

Camas grins. "I ask good ones."

"In our modern world today," Portman says, glancing around, "we face depression, immune diseases, cancer. What you see here is a slow food movement for a slow earth."

"So, what is slow?" Camas presses.

"Hopefully, you'll learn that this weekend." Portman bows slightly, eyes closed, then opens them with a warm smile. "So nice to meet you both. I'll see you tonight."

He walks away calmly through the chaos.

"I'm grabbing a pint," Camas says, suddenly. She darts off.

"I'll meet you in the room," Tilly calls.

Max raises an eyebrow. "See you later at the opening ceremony," he says, kissing Tilly on the cheek.

CHAPTER 18

Afghan Purple Carrot

(ENDANGERED)

Arrival Day

Keynote Address & Welcome Party

Day One: Slow

Greenwashed to Food Rx

"Synthetic medicine and synthetic ag are for sick people.
Pure food is for health"

Slow Farming Methods, Regenerative Farming, Seed Saving,

Organic, Biodynamic, Agroforestry/Syntropic Farming

~ There Is a Solution ~

Day Two: Slower

Land Back to Reparation Rebound

"My birthright is the earth, the sky, the wind, the water."

Land Finance, Farm Policy, Land Access, Regenerative Finance

Policies, Grants, Subsidies, Farm Bill, Reparation

~ How It Works ~

Day Three: Slowest
Healthy Heartbeats to Centenarian Bounties
"Real devotion is an unbroken receptivity to the truth."
Natural (Non-Pharma) Longevity, Centenarian Mini Memoirs,
Slow activism, Environmental Bill of Rights
~ Into Action ~

Camas sits near the back of the conference room. Tilly squeezes through the row, and Camas lifts her backpack off the seat beside her.

"Here's the schedule," Tilly whispers, handing her a leaf-shaped card made of plantable seed paper.

"We got that two weeks ago from Max," Camas whispers back.

"Baesamen is trying to get on the roster."

"What?!"

A woman with a green bandana in front of them turns and glares.

"Well, I won't have any trouble telling a joke before that chemical clown," Camas mutters. "What are we listening to? I thought this was the welcome party?"

"It's the opening keynote. I heard Max say 'welcome.'"

"Where's the party?"

"Shush," Green Bandana hisses.

"Give it a chance," Tilly says. "And, yes, shush."

Unintelligible words buzz from the stage.

"I've been giving it a chance. It's all mumbo jumbo. GMO studies this. Regen that." Camas pulls a flask from her bag.

"I thought you were taking a break. What's with the flask?"

"You've seen this flask."

"That was on our bikes. The party is in an hour. Social drinking. Not flask drinking."

"Judged." Camas takes a long swig and stows it. "Josh told me you called him."

"I did. I'm worried," Tilly whispers.

"You don't need to be."

Applause ripples through the room.

"Here comes Portman!" Tilly says.

Max jogs onto the stage and closes his eyes for a beat. Then he leaps into the air, hair flying. "Welcome to the Slow Earth Food Festival!!"

Cheers.

"First, let me introduce you to our MCs." Max points toward the back. "Tilly and Camas of One More Year. Please stand!"

They rise and wave. Applause.

"Now, let's welcome Ny Green, who'll introduce tonight's keynote." He steps aside as Ny enters to warm applause.

"Ny is the founder of Sereneway, the first agricultural housing development in an urban suburb."

Luxey claps wildly from the back beside Paignton.

"Thank you, Maximo. I love Burning Man! My camp had matching sarongs. Commando for the win."

Camas winces, blinks.

Max nods as he walks off.

"I know you're excited to hear from Portman Royal..."

More applause.

"...but I've been given a few minutes to tell you about Sereneway to I'll take it."

"Of course you will," Camas mutters.

"Shush. Ny was a kind host. I'm surprised you can even remember that night."

"That's harsh."

"I created Sereneway after watching my kids play in the country. Long walks, naps, growing food...it gave us peace. Then one day, a developer started cutting down trees by our house. I tried to stop it. Bought land around us. I had built a chain of pet stores, so I knew how to get things done. Within a year, I went from 120 acres to nearly a thousand. And that's how we started our 'sustainable agrihood.'"

Applause.

"Last month, I sat next to a gray-bearded man on a plane. Said he was a writer and farmer. I bragged about Sereneway...our farm parks, art installations, sustainable water system, the inn, food classes...blah, blah, blah. He nodded, listened. Eventually, he slept. When we landed, I realized I knew nothing about him."

Ny smiles. "So, I asked. He said, 'I make bread, clothing, and friendships, and I grow vegetables.'

'I do too,' I said.

'No, son,' he replied. 'You have a division of people. Those who provide life's essentials and those who use them.'

I said, 'Well...we're getting there.'

Then he asked, 'Could this Sereneway be everywhere? Would its duplication heal the planet?'

I wanted to say yes. I'm a salesman. But I couldn't lie. I said, 'No. Not enough land, money, water...or lithium, cobalt, manganese, nickel, or graphite...for everyone to drive from cities to agrihoods.'

Groans from the crowd.

"Then he said: 'The truth is the only real needs are food, shelter, and companionship. Everything else is a bonus. One who is content with that treads lightly and soon has something to give back. One who isn't, makes an awful ruckus in their time on this planet.'"

"Introduce Portman!!" Camas yells, slightly slurred.

"Shush!" Tilly says.

"And now," Ny smiles, "please welcome the man I met on that flight: Portman Royal!"

Portman Royal walks out in an indigo knit vest. He embraces Ny to applause, then steps forward.

"Thank you, Maximo. Thank you, Ny. And thank you all. We all have much to do."

Charlie films from the side of the room.

Pedro Primer moment: Pedro sits alert, looking over Lake Bijou Ness. "Woof. I interrupt this chapter—which may be getting a bit preachy—to let you know that when we take a deep breath and settle in to listen, we're often glad we did. And I promise: there's action coming next chapter. Food is life. Don't miss it."

"Farming," Portman says, "is a craft. We care more for the artisan than the product. And more for the quality than the quantity."

Murmers.

"I hear you. Some nodding, some unsure. It's confusing...because modern society is separated from the artisan farmer. The result? Suicides among mono-crop farmers. Illness among those eating the crops. I dislike euphemisms like 'big ag.' I prefer truth. A separation from the life force of plants is like depriving people of oxygen. Like a fish tossed onto land."

Applause.

"My friend Wendell Barry wrote, 'That one American farmer can now feed himself and fifty-six others may be a triumph of technology...but not of agriculture or culture. It's a trade of energy for knowledge, methodology for care, technology for morality.'"

More applause.

"This work is never done. As soon as the moon falls, here comes the sun."

He glances at Charlie.

"You are here because you are artisans. You grow, cook, support, and share food...not for riches, but for a beautiful life. That is economic nonviolence. A system that doesn't exploit. When we live with beautiful frugality...when the distance between the earth, our hands, and our mouths is short...we become artisans of our lives. And we will live in peace."

Applause swells.

Portman places his hands in prayer, bows, then exits.

Pedro lies down, resting his head on his front paws as the lake sparkles behind him. "Primer out."

Charlie taps his phone to stop the video. He texts Randy.

Camas glances at Tilly, who wipes her eyes. Camas hands her a tissue.

"Thanks."

"Come on. Let's hit the welcome party."

AquAdvantage™ Salmon

(GMO – AQUABOUNTY TECHNOLOGIES)

"There you are!" Tilly says. "I've been looking for you."

Camas is holding court in the hotel lobby, laughing loudly with a small group.

"Hey, sista, I've been enjoying the hard-farmed hand kombucha booth," Camas slurs in a loud voice.

"I think you mean 'hand-farmed hard kombucha," Tilly replies. "How many did you have?"

"Tilly, meet Fanny, Moonlight, and Orange-Tail."

"Nice to meet you," Tilly shakes their hands, polite but distracted. "Sorry to steal Camas. We need to prepare for tomorrow."

"Aww, I just met them! We can wing it." Camas says, wobbling slightly. Moonlight catches her arm.

"Whoops. Thanks!"

Camas looks back at Tilly, "Introducing Fanny Beautemps, owner of Blue Shepherdess Fields. She's speaking on day three and has a thousand Blue Cheese Lester sheep that she uses for fiber, fire control, and poop."

"I think you mean Blue Faced Leicester," Tilly says gently.

"And it's 300, not a thousand," Fanny adds with a smile.

"Aww shucks. How did you know that?"

"It's my farm?" Fanny replies.

"No, I meant Tilly."

"I studied the speakers," Tilly says. "Which is why we should go now."

Tilly takes Camas by the arm. "Nice meeting all of you. Looking forward to your talk, Fanny."

Camas waves as they head toward the elevator.

Cleo, Paul, Dubs, Hopper, Adofo, and Percy unload heavy bags of soil and an ice chest from Dubs' truck, setting everything beside the basketball court. Two basketballs rest near a neat row of shovels, trowels, and garden claws. Flats of leafy seedlings cover the picnic table under dappled morning light.

Paul kneels by the fence, painting bold black letters onto a wooden sign: Project Backboard. He drills holes into the top corners, threads wire through them, and carefully fastens the sign to the chain-link fence, taking care not to smudge his jersey.

Cleo steps back and hucks a basketball high over the court. It spins, arcs, and swishes clean through the net.

"Still got it," Cleo says, brushing soil from their palms.

Percy nods. "Next time, we build the garden and run the score."

"I need it," Cleo mutters. "My boss delivers stress like an overnight package. Sundays. On my doorstep or with a signature."

"We'll call it double overtime," Dubs adds, grinning.

They all laugh. Cleo pulls a trowel from the bag and begins digging into the corner bed of soil.

A small voice interrupts. "Can I help?"

They turn. A girl, maybe eleven, stands at the edge of the court holding a box of tomato starts.

"Damn!" Dubs jumps. "Where'd you come from?"

"A few blocks over. I told my mom I saw some old guys trying to garden, and she said to bring these."

"Who you calling old?" Adofo grins, patting his salt-and-pepper dreads.

"Thanks," Cleo says warmly. "Grab a trowel."

She sets the box down, kneels beside Cleo, and begins to dig.

The guys exchange glances. Then they all go back to planting.

"Hey, what's your name?" Cleo asks.

"Zaria."

"Well, Zaria, you just upgraded the whole crew. You and your friends are welcome anytime. We're out here Tuesdays, Thursdays, and Saturdays—before the courts open."

Zaria keeps her eyes on the soil. "I think other courts could use this too."

Cleo nods, voice low but sure. "Let's grow something different here. Real time, not screen time. Real food, not fake food."

The others nod. Percy turns up the music. Hands move in rhythm with the beats and the earth.

CHAPTER 20

Hampshire Lamb "Cool Whip"– Born 8.8 lbs. Slaughtered at 7 months, 81 lbs. – Hot carcass weight 44 lbs.

(NATURAL LIFESPAN 11 YEARS)

Day One: Slow

Greenwashed to Food Rx

"Synthetic medicine and synthetic ag are for sick people.
Pure food is for health."

Slow Farming Methods, Regenerative Farming, Seed Saving, Organic,

Biodynamic, Agroforestry/Syntropic Farming

~ There Is a Solution ~

A DJ plays upbeat music as eight children ages four to fourteen walk down the center aisle of the conference hall, each carrying a colorful basket of fruits, vegetables, and seeds. They line up on the stage. Max and Tilly stand on either end.

Tilly holds the mic to a seven-year-old girl.

"Monocropping is the agricultural practice of growing a single crop, such as corn or soybeans, year after year on the same land, with no crop rotation," the girl says. "The opposite of monocropping is diversity. Three plants we grow on our farm are Red of Florence onions, Puma peppers, and Marian rutabagas."

Applause.

Max holds the mic and whispers, "Your turn," to an eleven-year-old boy named Leif.

He speaks confidently. "Monocultures don't exist in nature. Even forests that look like all pines have layers of other species underneath. Three plants we grow are Corrales Azafran safflower, Green Giant tomatoes, and Yamato Cream watermelon."

Applause.

Another child steps forward.

"Biological diversity is critical for the health of the soil as it provides an assortment of vitamins and minerals in the food we eat. Three plants we grow are Love Parade yarrow, Glass Gem corn, and Kyoto Red carrots."

"Seventy-five percent of the world's crop varieties have been lost over the last century. Three of the plants my family's farm grows are Purple Lady bok choy, Indian snake beans, and Lime basil."

Camas walks onto the stage, surprising the kids.

"Wow!" she says.

They freeze mid-smile.

"The stat about the loss of crops is so sad," Camas says. "We need some jokes now! Hey kids, why did the farmer want to bury all of his money?"

Max joins in with a grin. "We don't know, Camas. Why did the farmer want to bury all of his money?"

"To make the soil rich!"

The kids giggle. The audience laughs.

"Carry on!" Camas waves them forward.

Tilly holds the mic for the next child.

"There are 442 million acres of monocropping in the U.S. alone. Three of the plants we grow are Boston pickling cucumbers, Orange Spice jalapeños, and Monstruex De Viroflay spinach," a young girl says with a French accent.

"That's easy for you to say!" Max jokes.

The next child speaks. "Only nine plant species account for almost two-thirds of total crop production. Three plants we grow at our farm are Chinese Red Meat radishes, King Tut Purple peas, and Alaskan Red Shades nasturtium."

Tilly kneels with the mic in front of a four-year-old boy.

The little boy says, "Over the past ten years, we've had 100 million tons of herbicides dumped onto our crops, polluting our soil and streams."

The crowd groans.

"They're groaning about the chemicals, not you. You're doing great," Tilly whispers.

The boy grins and raises his basket. "My family grows Gelber En-squisher Custard squash, Vulcan sparkle chard, and purple armadillos."

The crowd claps. The kids beam.

The last speaker steps up, a tall, poised fourteen-year-old girl. She looks down at the little boy. "That's my brother, and he meant tomatillos, not armadillos."

Laughter from the audience.

"Large quantities of synthetic herbicides, insecticides, bactericides, and fertilizers are used in monocropping. Three plants we grow without chemicals are Barry's Crazy Cherry tomatoes, Tall Jacks kale, and Autumn Buckskin pumpkins."

Max throws his arms open. "Amazing! Thank you so much!"

Tilly adds, "So full of hope! I'm hungry and it's only 9:30 am!"

She leads the children offstage as the audience cheers.

"Wasn't that the cutest thing? The kids and veggies part. Not the mono mutante monster cropping!" Camas says.

A pause.

"How 'bout another joke?" Camas grins. "I'll keep it clean since the kids are still here. What's a scarecrow's favorite fruit?"

Max plays along. "I don't know, Camas...what's a scarecrow's favorite fruit?"

One of the farm kids calls back from the aisle, "Straw-berries!"

"That's right!" Camas laughs. "And pesticide-free ones, of course!"

The crowd chuckles.

CHAPTER 21

Pink Plume Celery

(ENDANGERED)

Tilly and Camas make their rounds through the festival booths. There are seeds, prepared foods, marinades, jams, chutneys, and heirloom varieties of grains, vegetables, and fruits. Food artisans carve intricate designs into watermelons, squash, and gourds. They pass by small farm equipment: no-till seed drills, broadforks, weed torches, wire hoes, wheelbarrows, rakes, shovels, spades, and pruners. Signage, brochures, and digital screens showcase spiritual, natural, organic, and biodynamic methods, alongside phrases like zero-budget natural farming, syntropic, and agroforestry.

Tilly pauses under a display of Opinel harvest knives under a sign that reads *Swiss Alps 1890*.

They stop to listen to a couple playing fiddle and banjo, and chat with exhibitors and attendees. Across the tent is a Baesamen booth with a floor banner: *We Sell Obviate Science, SOS. Exciting Festival Announcement!*

"Hey, all this talking is getting me thirsty. I'm grabbing a beer," Camas says, walking off.

Tilly continues. A few attendees smile at her as she passes.

"Great job," a man says.

"I like your hair," a young girl adds, handing Tilly a daisy chain on a silk cord.

"Thank you," Tilly says, kneeling so the girl can tie it around her head.

Tilly approaches a booth filled with baskets of fruits and vegetables and a sign that reads *Veg-Health Meter*.

Joss, wearing a white lab coat, stands before a group. "The bionutrient meter is actually quite simple. It uses LED lights that bounce off a fruit or vegetable. Some light is absorbed; the rest bounces back. The sensor reads that difference."

Behind her, a large display reads *Nutrient Variation in the Food Supply*, showing a circle of produce with visible gaps between the most and least nutritious.

Tilly studies it. "Wow, does that mean what I think it means?"

"If you think it means that you'd need to eat fifteen of the least nutritious grapes from the supermarket to get the nutrition of one high-quality grape, then yes," Joss says, offering her hand. "I'm Joss."

"Tilly. Nice to meet you." They shake hands. "So, the best beets are nine times more nutritious than the worst?"

"That's right. Potatoes are six times. Zucchini five."

"What are you tracking?"

"We measure nutrients essential to human health... calcium, iron, potassium, magnesium, zinc, sulfur, antioxidants, and polyphenols."

"Polyphenols?" Tilly questions.

Camas reappears, holding a beer. "Chocolate and wine!"

Joss laughs. "Exactly. There are around 8,000 polyphenols found naturally in plants. They're antioxidants. They help neutralize free radicals...those that cause cancer, diabetes, and heart disease."

"Beer's got polyphenols," Camas says, raising her beer.

"Joss, this is Camas," Tilly says.

"Hi, Camas." Joss smiles. "That's true. Ideally, this device ends up in the hands of consumers. If you could choose the blueberries for your children that were eight times more nutritious, wouldn't you?"

"Absolutely," Tilly agrees.

"Tilly has a bun in the oven," Camas says, pointing.

"Congratulations!"

"Thanks... and thanks for working on this."

"Of course," Joss responds.

Tilly scans Joss's QR code. She notices a stack of postcards showing a tranquil lakeside campground, framed by oaks, hickories, black walnuts, and cottonwoods. The card reads *Vegan Campout, Lake Keomah State Park.*

"I think I heard about this. I wish I could go."

"We are not biking to that lake," Camas says flatly.

"Ethics, diet, or planet?" Joss asks.

"Excuse me?"

"Why are you vegan?"

"Ethics, I guess," Tilly answers. "I was about five when I told my mom I wasn't going to eat animals, but she didn't listen. I stopped fully six years ago. You?"

"I'm a food scientist. First, it was health. Lower meat consumption reduced my risk of stroke, cancer, and heart disease. Then I learned the climate data."

"Deforestation and methane?" Camas chimes in.

"Exactly. And cruelty. That's still the hardest part."

"It's the all-or-nothing dilemma," Camas says.

"What do you mean?" Joss asks.

"Our subconscious mind fears that if we look at one thing too closely, we'll have to look at everything," Tilly explains.

"Yeah. That...and I'm selfish. I kept eating meat because it felt too hard to change," Camas admits.

"There's a reason the campout is at Lake Keowah. They're planning a protest at a major pork slaughterhouse. USDA found that 15,000 pigs had paddle marks and other wounds," Joss says.

Tilly winces. "Awful."

"Bastards," Camas mutters.

"I let myself feel it now," Joss says, wiping a tear. "I don't like it, but it's a part of being human."

"Are you going to the campout?" Tilly asks gently.

"I can't. But, I'm working on some things in the lab to help the cause."

"Good for you. I scanned your card...let's stay in touch." Tilly hugs her.

"Let's," Joss agrees.

Camas raises a hand. "High five for the veggie zapper?"

They connect palms and laugh.

"Yes, I got the video of Father Time and the munchkins, God dammit!" Bruno yells.

"Just checking, sir," Cleo says, placing coffee on his desk.

Bruno scrolls with a furrowed brow.

"Is there anything else you need?" Cleo asks.

"Need?! Yes, there's something I effin need!"

"What is that, sir?"

"I need this medieval mess of a gathering, this, this joke...shut down! His face reddens. "This miserable attempt to take us back to a time when..."

"When people grew their own food, sir?"

Bruno glares. "Big ag grows food now. People don't need to dig in the dirt and stand in the hot sun. Push a button, get a robot instead. That's progress. Who'd want to torture themselves with their hands in the dirt like that?"

"You wouldn't want to."

"That's right! I was worried you'd turned on me."

"You wouldn't want to...especially not in soil laced with chemical leftovers from old wars" Cleo says.

"Aha! I knew it. You're one of them! What are you going to do? Start a farm in your overalls like Captain Fantastic?"

"Maybe."

"Careful, Cleo. I pay you too much to go crunchie."

Bruno scrolls quickly. "There. There it is!"

"What?"

"The bug."

"The what?"

"The monster bug to shut this festival and every farm-to-fork fantasy down."

"I haven't heard of any outbreaks."

"You won't. Not until I leak the story. I don't need an outbreak here. I just need one poor country to say it's spreading. With enough hush money, anything's possible."

Cleo is silent.

"Sales meeting. Tomorrow. Zoom. 7:00 Central."

"OK," Cleo says, turning.

"Cleo...one more thing."

"Yes?"

"Can I trust you?"

Cleo doesn't answer. They stare at the glass eyes of the taxidermy lion. They turn around. "You want to know after nine and a half years if you can trust me?"

"Answer the question."

"You can trust me," they say. Cleo walks out. Under their breath, "To do the right thing."

Tilly and Camas walk the carpeted hall of the conference hotel after a long day.

Tilly bumps into two petite women exiting a meeting room. "Oh, I'm so sorry!"

She looks up. "Perla! Frida! You've met!"

Tilly hugs them. Camas hugs Frida, a striking Native American elder with soft, weathered skin and long gray hair.

"Perla, this is Camas."

"Amazing job today, you two," Perla says. She smiles at Camas. "You're very funny."

"Thanks," Camas replies.

Tilly and Camas glance into the meeting room. Inside, a gorgeous Indian tent glows with lanterns over a long table. The guests, mostly silver-haired, speak in calm tones. Max is among them.

"What are you doing in there?" Camas asks.

"We can't say," Frida replies

Camas narrows her eyes. "Max made the cool list. I object."

"He was invited by Portman Royal," Frida says.

"Portman's here?" Tilly peers in. "I'd love to speak with him again."

"He's already gone. Maybe tomorrow," Frida says.

"Am I chopped liver?" Perla teases.

"Never. I've missed you," Tilly says, hugging her. She turns to Frida. "And I've missed you too, though it's only been a few weeks."

"I miss you too, dear one," Frida says.

Perla sighs. "I've been busy trying to hold back the planet's scalding. Iceland is feeling it faster than most."

"Whatever's happening in that room, it looks important. Maybe we can help," Tilly offers.

Perla pauses, glancing behind her. "We're meeting each night. Let me ask the Elders... uh, others...if we can include you."

"If it's meant to be," Tilly says, squeezing Perla's hand.

"Good luck tomorrow. I hear tomorrow's topics go even deeper."

"That's the goal. Slow. Slower. Slowest." Tilly smiles.

"If we're going to slow this thing down, we'll need to create a goddamn ruckus," Camas says, then waves. "Hey, I see someone. I'll meet you in the room. Frida, nice seeing you. Perla, nice to meet you."

Camas heads off.

Perla watches her go. "She'd be funnier without the alcohol."

"You could tell?" Tilly asks.

"I've been to enough rock concerts."

"I thought I was the only one."

"Her fire has always burned bright," Frida says. "Some people dim their own fire."

CHAPTER 22

Plum – prunus domestica

(GMO – United States Department of Agriculture)

Day Two: Slower

Land Back to Reparation Rebound

"My birthright is the earth, the sky, the wind, the water."

Land Finance, Farm Policy, Land Access, Regenerative Finance

Policies, Grants, Subsidies, Farm Bill, Land Back, Reparation

~ How It Works ~

"Where's Camas?" Max whispers to Tilly.

They stand on the conference center patio overlooking the wide river, the crowd gathering in clusters around them, several hundred festivalgoers in various states of caffeination and sunhat orientation.

"She was moving slowly this morning," Tilly replies, tense. "She promised she'd be on time."

She checks her phone. "It's 9:03. We should start."

Max gives a small shrug, then faces the crowd with his signature beaming smile and warm eyes.

"Good morning from the banks of the majestic Mississippi River! Before we dive into today's presentations on Land Back, reparation movements, and the policies that shape our food systems, please welcome Tilly with a few words."

"Welcome to Day Two of the festival!" Tilly calls out.

Applause ripples through the patio.

"I want to begin by acknowledging the native peoples of this land. We are gathered on the traditional, ancestral, and unceded territory of the Báxoje (Bah Kho-je), Sauk, and Meskwaki peoples. We honor their Elders -- past and present, and future. Our very presence here today reflects the ongoing exclusion and erasure of Indigenous peoples and the violation of multiple treaties."

The crowd claps, solemn and strong.

"Thank you. I'm honored to welcome Kanienten:hawi, who will be teaching a seed-saving class later today."

Applause grows louder as a calm, grounded woman steps forward.

"Thank you, Tilly and Max," Kanienten:hawi begins.

Camas stumbles into place beside them, a bit breathless. Tilly shoots a look.

Camas mouths, "Sorry."

Kanienten:hawi smiles, unbothered. "I was born in a snowstorm. My paternal Mohawk grandmother gave me my name: Kanienten:hawi, which means 'she brings the snow.' You can call me Kani.

I live in Northern California and am part of a growing movement to reconnect seeds and humans to the land. Seed rematriation returns seeds to their place of origin and to the care of those who once tended them. We avoid worn-out, establishment words such as food systems."

"Whoops, sorry," Max says, with a sheepish grin.

"It's OK, Max." Kani's voice is gentle. "We prefer words like foodways. And we often replace the word food with seeds. So food security becomes seed security. Food sovereignty becomes seed sovereignty. You feel that? It brings the conversation down to earth...makes it tangible, actionable."

People nod. A few call out, "Yes!"

Camas leans into the mic. "Big ag wants it to be vague."

Kani nods. "That's right, Camas. We deny those who try to separate us from the seeds. Rematriation is a sacred return, a feminine force, named across spiritual traditions, binding us to the seeds and the soil. This is Indigenous wisdom. And it is human wisdom."

She lowers her head.

The audience follows her into stillness.

Tilly and Max bow their heads. Camas fidgets, peeking at the sky, then follows suit.

After a long breath, Kani lifts her gaze. "Thank you. I hope you'll join me for the seed-saving demonstration later today. It's not just a class...it's an invitation to apprentice yourself to the seeds."

"Yes, we'll be there!" Tilly says, beaming. "Thank you, Kani!"

Inside the main conference hall, hundreds of attendees gather as three jumbotron screens power on. The title "Manifest Destiny Unwound" appears, followed by a film montage of Land Back victories and hard-won lessons.

A narrator begins:

"Land Back contains cultural, spiritual, and political meanings. Some Indigenous communities resist the term altogether...why should they have to buy what was already theirs?"

The screen shifts to the Black Hills of South Dakota.

"Pe' Sla is sacred to the Lakota. In a rare effort, the Rosebud Sioux Tribe repurchased nearly 2,000 acres of this holy site. According to legend, it's where the Morning Star placed the souls of seven women into the Pleiades constellation."

The audience sits in focused quiet as more stories unfold.

"The Bois Forte Band of Chippewa... The Yurok Tribe... Nunavut's historic reclamation... Nearly three million acres returned under modern claims."

Images roll by...intercropped farms, ceremonial fires, elders, and youth planting seeds.

Then, a brief comedic scene appears from a well-known TV show.

An older white couple drives through the countryside. The husband squints at a spray-painted billboard that reads "Land Back."

"What do you suppose that means?" he asks.

His wife shrugs. They banter. He's confused, wondering if they mean all of the land.

She nods, deadpan. "They deserve it."

He sputters something about the casinos. She calls him a shit-ass.

The festival crowd bursts into cheers.

Fade to black.

CHAPTER 23

Roundup Ready™ Soybean – Glycine max L.

(GMO - MONSANTO)

Camas steps up to the mic. "Wow. So inspiring! That reminds me of land acknowledgments. Tilly did one this morning for this land. Thank you, Tilly."

The audience applauds.

"But when you think about it, it's kind of strange we do those, isn't it? I mean...WTF...who is that really helping?"

Some in the audience look surprised.

"Picture this: I rob your house, move in, and then each night, I light a candle, close my eyes, and whisper, 'I want to acknowledge that this living room is stolen...' And then I go watch Netflix."

A ripple of nervous laughter runs through the crowd. Some are silent.

"Thanks for laughing along. We laugh so we don't cry, right?"

Tilly walks up, smiling.

"Here's Tilly to introduce our next speakers," Camas says.

"Thanks for speaking the truth, friend."

Camas gives Tilly the thumbs-up and steps aside.

"Our next speakers are three women from India, Mexico, and Canada, leading the charge in seed sovereignty and fighting for agriculture free of poison and GMOs. First, please help me welcome Dr. Vandana Shiva, a world-renowned environmental thinker, activist, feminist, science philosopher, and writer."

The crowd applauds loudly.

"Thank you, Tilly and Camas, and everyone here at the Slow Earth Food Festival. I'm honored to introduce my good friend and fellow seed warrior, Francesca Luz Lopez."

Applause.

"I've spent over thirty years defending small farmers around the world. The Navdanya, or 'nine seeds,' movement was born as a response to corporations trying to patent and profit from nature."

Boos roll through the crowd.

"These companies use intellectual property laws and so-called 'free trade' agreements to bully our people and governments. We've fought biopiracy and their attempts to patent thousands of years of nature and Indigenous knowledge. This includes the Neem tree, our basmati rice, and our ancient wheat varieties. Indian wheat – like Mexico's corn – is the result of generations of care and innovation. But Baesamen and others claim they 'invented' these seeds and falsify patents. We've proven it...and we fight on."

Applause.

"I am thrilled to introduce Francesca Luz Lopez, who will share how Mexico is standing up to the U.S. government to protect its corn, its culture, and its people. Please welcome Francesca."

Francesca joins Vandana, and they hug. A vibrant sideshow appears: colorful cornfields, a map of Mexico shaded in brilliant corn kernels, and in bold letters: Sin maíz no hay país.

"Thank you, Vandana. Hello everyone!" Francesca waves to the audience. "I was invited by Portman Royal because he thought that our work might resonate with you. Mexico is protecting its maize gene pool and cultural heritage, including traditional Mexican gastronomy, which is recognized by UNESCO as a world heritage site. We defend Indigenous and peasant communities who keep this seed legacy alive. It's a living, evolving system that now faces real threats from GMO maize."

Applause.

"Baesamen, Syndown, and others claim Mexico's decision isn't based on science. That's false. Our comprehensive response includes hundreds of academic studies showing cause for concern: direct health risks, epigenetic changes passed to future generations, increased antibiotic resistance, and reduced nutritional content."

She pauses and takes a breath.

"Whew. Dios mío. It's a lot to take in. Sometimes we may ask ourselves...are we making too big a deal out of this?"

The screen shifts: 56 ears of genetically diverse Mexican corn, A to Z, from Ancho, Apacity, Arrocillo, Azul to Zamarano Amarillo, Zapalote Chico, Zapalote Grande.

The crowd gasps at their beauty.

"And then I remember. These GMO products weren't created to nourish us. They were created for money."

The crowd boos.

"We can't let corporations bully us. They frame Mexico as a lone resistor. But in truth, we stand with the global majority. Data shows there's no worldwide preference for GMOs. At least 40 countries have imposed full or partial restrictions, most banning GMO planting altogether."

Applause.

"In the U.S., over 90% of corn grown is GMO. It's turned into high fructose corn syrup used in sodas, cereals, and processed foods. These foods are linked to fatty liver, high blood sugar, and type 2 diabetes. Most GMO corn here doesn't even feed people. It feeds cattle. And you eat that too."

The crowd murmurs.

"Mexico is a major producer of white corn without GMOs. We hope to be a light in the fight against these toxic predators."

The crowd stands and claps.

Francesca calls, "Guarda la semilla! Save our seeds!"

The crowd joins her. "Guarda la semilla! Save our seeds!"

Francesa stands back, smiling.

As applause rolls across the conference hall, Luxey meanders toward the catering table and grabs a vegan cupcake with mango frosting. She takes a dainty bite, then notices a trio of ceramic bowls beside the desserts, each one filled with heirloom maize.

She leans in. One bowl glows with muted reds and golds.

"Zapalote Chico?" says a voice beside her.

She turns. Paignton looks down at her, holding a compostable cup of horchata.

"No, it's Pisinkalla," she says, pointing to a poster of Mexican corn over the table. "Is that dirt on your fingers?"

"I can always find some soil to tend," Paignton smiles.

Luxey whispers to the maize kernels. "You got this."

Paignton chuckles. "Seed whisperer."

"Just a little encouragement."

He nods toward the stage. "That Francesca sure seems to have their back too. But we all could use a little cheer squad."

An elder woman with soft grey curls and glasses walks onto stage, clapping in time. "Guarda la semilla. Save our seeds!"

"Please welcome my friend Lova Saskatoon from Canada!" Francesca says, hugging her.

Lova takes the mic. "I come from the land of rape and honey."

The crowd goes silent.

"My town is considering changing that slogan. And yes, it refers to rapeseed, canola, not the other kind of rape. But I think the slogan should stay!"

A few startled murmurs.

"Why? Not for pride. Not for Lain roots. But because rape... is what's been done to our seeds."

A beat. Then loud applause.

"The rape began in 1998. Baesamen sued my husband, Pierson, and me for half a million dollars after our fields were contaminated by their GMO seeds. A long legal fight followed. We were harassed and threatened. We were once at Cape Town Parliament when a Baesamen rep shook his fist and said, 'Nobody stands up to us. We'll destroy you.'"

Gasps from the crowd.

"But we stood our ground. In the end, they agreed to pay for the cost of removing their GMO plants from our field. It was less than $1,000 Canadian, but set a precedent: if your farm is contaminated, they're liable."

The audience applauds.

"We still have work to do. Pierson used to say, 'GMOs were never about feeding the world. They're about controlling the seed supply. Control that, and you control the food supply. If farmers lose seed rights, we go back to a feudal system, just with corporations instead of kings.'"

Lova closes her eyes for a second.

"My Pierson. Rest his soul."

Francesca and Vandana return to the stage with her. Camas and Tilly join them.

Vandana reaches out. They all clasp hands.

"When we use the term women, we speak to the feminine force in all beings," Vandana says strongly. "Now is the time to reject the war-based model of agriculture. Now is the time to let women and nature lead us...to farming that works with the earth, not against it. Women and Indigenous people, the true scientists of regeneration, are growing more food with more biodiversity by partnering with life itself."

The audience listens, still and charged.

"We resist monocultures of the mind. We choose freedom. Our utopia is growing gardens. Our power is in partnership with the earth and each other. Now is the time to let women lead the way!"

Thunderous applause. The women embrace and wave.

Bruno watches the live feed in his office...Vandana, Francesca, Lova, Tilly, Camas, holding hands on stage, the crowd roaring.

Bruno slams the laptop shut, yanks open a drawer, and pulls out maroon leather boxing gloves.

His jaw clenched, face flushed, he jams on the gloves, tightens the Velcro, throws a few stiff punches into the heavy bag.

Then winds up...and slugs the stuffed lion in the face. It collapses with a thud.

CHAPTER 24

American Pekin Duck "Whitney"- Born 1.6 oz Slaughtered at 8 weeks, 9.5 lbs. – Hot carcass weight 4.9 lbs.

(NATURAL LIFESPAN 10 YEARS)

"Frida! I'm so happy to see you."

Frida sits down next to Tilly under the festival tent, placing a plate with a black bean quesadilla, avocado, onions, and salsa beside Tilly's bowl of ancient grain quinoa salad with olives, carrots, onions, raw sesame seeds, and arugula.

"Likewise, mother, sister, daughter, friend."

Tilly smiles.

"How have you been feeling during your travels?" Frida asks, putting a hand gently on Tilly's belly.

"Fine. My dreams have been interesting."

"I'm sure."

"Any advice from the ancestors?"

"When my mother was pregnant, there was a long list of wives' tales handed down to us, like wear your hair down and don't pick out a name before birth."

"Those don't seem so bad."

"I suppose not. How about this one? 'A baby should not be allowed to cross her fingers, or the mother will have another one right away.'"

"Oh my. No finger crossing!"

Frida laughs. "You and Camas can join us this evening after the conference. Seven o'clock."

"That's so great. Same room?"

"Yes."

"Thank you, Frida."

Frida is quiet for a moment, then says softly, "Your baby is still in the spiritual realm. Listen well to those dreams."

"Where'd the tent come from? Looks like the Elders' tent from Burning Man," Camas whispers to Max.

"When they invited me, I suggested a tent."

"Definitely adds ambiance."

"Tent of meeting."

"Huh?"

"A tent of meeting... where Moses would go to talk to God."

"I see a bunch of Native Americans, not Jews."

"But can you feel God?"

Camas glances upward at the ornate ceiling of the Indian wedding tent, then downward toward the massive table ringed with eighty participants: Native Elders and tribal chairpersons, Hani, Perla, Frida, Vandana Shiva, and Portman Royal. Women outnumber men by three to one. Sage, sweetgrass, and cedar burn in abalone-shaped clay bowls in the corners.

Camas shrugs. "I see a lot of old people. Just missing my happy hour."

Frida stands and taps her glass with a smooth, round stone.

"Silence, please." She turns to Hani.

"Let us begin," Hani says with quiet authority. She nods to two men who begin drumming and chanting a low rhythmic song.

Hani stands. "Let's begin this session of Seeds Over-Soul with a prayer from The Plains Tribe, taught to me by Iowan Elder José Hobday. Sister José was of the Seneca tribe and a modern Franciscan nun who has left her human form but joins us in spirit. Please pick up the prayer card at your place and step back from the table."

The group stands and takes a couple of steps backward.

"Take one step forward."

The group steps forward.

"Now, look all around the room," Hani says slowly. "Then up, then down."

The participants observe silently.

"O Great Spirit, we take this step in the day you have given. We embrace all we see—the season, the wind, the fragrances, the weather. All together..."

Max holds the card out in front of Camas. They read along.

"Let us always accept the day with a grateful heart."

"Take another step forward," Hani says. "O Spirit of Life, we put our arms around ourselves, all that we are, all that we can be. We stand here in our own histories, with all of our mistakes and victories. We hold all those we will meet in our journeying and our work. We will walk gently on this earth. All together…"

The group chants, "Let us walk gently through the lives of our companions, friends, and other living things. Though they make way for our passing, may they spring back, neither broken nor bruised."

"Take another step forward."

The group complies.

"O glorious Spirit of Mystery, we put our arms around you. We do not know what will happen to us on this journey, but we accept it. All together…"

Voices join together. "Give us a heart of courage and believing, so we may put our trust in you and fear nothing."

The drums and chanting end. Hani turns to Frida and nods. Everyone sits.

Frida begins, "We have assembled again this evening to consider the events of today's festival and to forward the work of the seed savers. Please welcome Tilly and Camas this evening. They are interested in helping."

Voices from around the room echo, "Welcome."

Frida continues, "Tilly and Camas, we call ourselves Seeds Over-Soul. We are a group of seed-saver warriors, some public, others clandestine…intent on saving sacred, ancient, heritage, and modern natural seeds and their peoples. We represent communities across the nation and world."

"Holy cow," Camas mutters.

Some laugh.

Portman continues, "It is a small miracle we come together. We are fiercely independent. But, we agree that the topic of seed saving is critical. There are great threats to the future of good seeds and good food. By joining forces, we protect past work that strengthens what's ahead."

Camas squints at Perla. "Besides me, one of these things is not like the others. Why are you here?"

"That's right, Camas," Hani responds. "Most of us live on Turtle Island. Perla?"

Perla chuckles. "Good question. As Prime Minister of Iceland, I was invited to sit on the board of the Svalbard Global Seed Vault in Norway."

"Isn't that the huge doomsday vault?" Camas asks.

"That's the one. Since 2008, it's taken in over a million seed acquisitions, representing about 13,000 years of agricultural history."

"Holy shit."

Tilly interjects. "Is that where this group stores its seeds?"

Perla shakes her head. "Some, but our banks are living seed banks. Seeds for long-term saving, but more importantly, seeds for living. We operate a network of under-the-radar seed banks. One reason we're here is to find more locations."

"Locations more accessible to everyday farmers around the globe," Vandana says.

"It's challenging," Hani says, "because seeds need climate-controlled storage."

"And the climate isn't helping," Portman adds.

"Why don't you use the Indian casino vaults?" Camas blurts.

Tilly looks at Camas.

"I mean Native casino vaults," Camas corrects.

The room pauses.

A tribal chairman breaks the silence, "Seeds stored with chips and cash?!"

"Wouldn't be big enough," another adds.

"Farmers and gamblers?" someone asks.

Loud discussion erupts.

Frida listens quietly, rubbing her stone between thumb and forefinger. Then taps her glass.

"Smallpox or the new buffalo?" she says. "We struggle to come to terms with our casinos and that paradox. Wouldn't protection of seeds under the same roof be an elegant solution?"

"And one with serious potential," Hani agrees. "There are over 500 casinos across the U.S."

"And non-casino tribes could serve as Seeds Over-Soul distribution pods," someone calls out.

The room buzzes with ideas.

Max turns to Camas, "Guess you did feel God."

Camas leans past him to Tilly, "I gotta go, sista. I've got some people to meet."

Charlie walks along the Mississippi River, the festival tent behind him as the sun dips low. He answers his phone.

"Hey, Dad."

Peter drives a dusty country road. "Some guys came out and installed the gadgets on the Hageman Ranch. Didn't even call me first."

"Sorry. Probably my fault. Now just go to the app store and..."

"I'm not going to any god-forsaken app floor... or store... or whatever the hell it is. Just wanted you to know."

"I'll handle it when I'm back."

"Whatever. How's the festival?"

"It's eye-opening."

"How's that?"

"I might be on the wrong team."

Silence.

"Dad?"

"You're a free agent, son."

CHAPTER 25

Cauley Apple

(ENDANGERED)

"Hey!" Camas, bleary-eyed, bounds into the hotel room and throws her backpack on the bed.

Tilly looks up from her laptop from her bed. "Where have you been? It's 3:10 in the morning."

"You're up too," Camas slurs. "I was with some friends."

Camas stumbles into the bathroom, grabs toothpaste and her toothbrush, and makes a couple of sloppy attempts to wet the brush under the running water. Eventually, she gets it into her mouth and starts brushing.

"I know you've been partying," Tilly calls out, "but I have a question for you."

"Shoot," Camas says around a mouthful of toothpaste. She leans in the doorway, white foam oozing from the corner of her mouth.

"What made you change your mind about eating meat?"

Camas wipes her mouth with her forearm, thinking. "First, it was just a thought, a possibility. Then, I made a different choice that evening at Ny's agri-estate. That was it. There was no burning bush."

"Hmmm."

"What are you doing up so late?" Camas peels off her clothes, pulls on an oversized T-shirt, and climbs into bed.

"I spoke with Max and Portman after the Seeds Over-Soul session. We're talking about changing tomorrow's agenda to focus on plants."

"Haven't we been talking about plants?"

"Versus meat."

"What?! There are quite a few farmers here with animals, and they don't all end up in a sweater vest. Some end up in the Mulligatawny."

"Exactly."

"Is this the right time and place?"

"If not now, when?"

Camas growns and pulls on a satin eye mask. "Someplace where we won't be driven out of town. Berkeley?" She falls back into bed.

"Where's my feisty friend? Soaked in bourbon?"

"Hey, it was a long day."

Tilly's voice sharpens. "How can we talk about saving the seeds, saving the soil, saving the planet...if we aren't saving animals?!"

Camas finishes yawning. "True."

"Mulligatawny started as a vegetarian dish in India. The British added the meat."

Camas, barely awake, "You're going to talk about stew?"

"Maybe I will," Tilly says defiantly. "A delicious French Basque Piperade, a Ratatouille, a nice Greek Tourlou, a Spanish Tombet or

Pisto, an Italian Ciambotta, a delicious Armenian pumpkin Ghapama."

"I smoked some weed. No more food talk. You're making me hungry."

"All without meat. Come to think of it, any stew can be delicious without meat."

"But is it delicious without livelihood?"

Tilly is silent.

Camas speaks slowly, half-asleep, "And your people will hang it on culture."

Tilly looks over at her, then turns back to her laptop and begins typing again.

CHAPTER 26

Whippersnapper Tomato

(ENDANGERED)

Day Three: Slowest

Healthy Heartbeats to Centenarian Bounties

"Real devotion is an unbroken receptivity to the truth."

Natural (Non-Pharma) Longevity, Centenarian Mini Memoirs,

Slow Activism, Environmental Bill of Rights

~ Into Action ~

"Where are you?" Cleo asks, sitting at Bruno's desk.

"I'm at the smelly earth festival. I flew in last night when I saw the bullshit that's going on here."

"I'm surprised you booked your own flight."

"Call Red Glatze and set a meeting for us."

"I doubt I can get him to St. Louis again."

"I'll go to Chocolate City."

"Excuse me?"

"Dubuque to DC late afternoon today. Book it."

A fluffy-headed Highland calf rubs against Bruno's leg. He turns to see an elderly woman leading the baby cow.

"And find me a celebrity who loves hamburgers!" he snaps. "Did you get that?"

"DC, celebrity burger-eater. Got it." Cleo hangs up.

Bruno feels warmth on his foot. He looks down. There's a pile of cow dung smeared on his two-thousand-dollar calfskin Alessandro Démesure Patchwork oxfords.

Max walks onto the festival stage, long dark hair flowing over a gold silk jacket. The crowd cheers.

He grins, gesturing to aboriginal-style paint on his face. "Like my face painting? Kara, from Heather Dove Farm, did it this morning."

Applause.

"We have a slight change to today's schedule," Max says.

Murmurs in the crowd.

"These past two days have been full of love...for the earth, for food, for each other. You've endured Camas's bad food jokes ..."

Camas mock-gasps from stage left.

"...and learned from Indigenous stories, slow farming practices, and soil healers. Now we ask you to keep an open mind...just as you've asked the world to do for your work."

"What's the change?!!" a festival-goer shouts out.

Tilly steps to the mic. "Today, we'll be talking about how to live to 100. In just a bit, you'll hear from centenarians themselves."

Applause.

She continues. "We've covered many elements of a long life, but we've adjusted today's agenda just a bit."

A slide appears behind her:

Day Three: Slowest

~~***Healthy***~~ ***Bloodless*** ~~***Heartbeats***~~***beets*** **to Centenarian Bounties**

"Real devotion is an unbroken receptivity to the truth."

Animals Bill of Rights, Natural Non-Pharma Longevity,

Centenarian Mini-Memoirs, Slow Activism

~ Into Action ~

Grumbling rises in the crowd. A couple stands, grabs their bags, and heads for the exit.

Tilly speaks quickly. "We understand this is unexpected. For those of you with young children, the content may be intense. We're streaming live on the festival website if you'd prefer to watch from another space."

Two mothers nod and exit with their toddlers.

Max adds, "For animal farmers or others who feel this isn't for you, we'll refund your tickets. But we do hope you'll stay."

People near the front shake their heads and walk out. Dozens follow, but some pause, turn, and return to their seats.

Tilly raises her voice. "Twelve million Africans were shipped to the New World in chains. A U.S. Army colonel said, 'Every dead buffalo is an Indian gone.' 40 million bison were slaughtered. A hundred thousand dolphins are still killed annually, often herded into coves to die. Six million Jews were murdered in the Holocaust. Since 1900, genocide has claimed 170 million lives. That's 75 million after we promised 'never again.'"

A door slams. More walk out. Others standing in the back sit down again.

"You may ask how a dolphin relates to a slave, or why I dare mention buffalo and the Holocaust in the same breath. But I ask you to consider: Is there a link between human brutality and our normalization of animal slaughter?"

Murmers spread.

"Captain Paul Watson said, 'If you want to know where you would have stood on slavery before the Civil War, don't look at where you stand today. Look at where you stand on animal rights.'"

A gray-bearded man in a shirt reading grass-fed shouts, "What does this have to do with farming?!"

"I appreciate the question," Tilly responds.

The screen behind her lights up.

26,193,533,721

The number climbs by thousands per second.

26,193,537,903 ...

26,193,540,014 ...

26,193,543,289 ...

Below it: *Scan Me* and a QR code.

"This is the Animal Kill Clock and the number of animals killed in the U.S. so far this year. Not including those who died pre-slaughter, over eight billion land animals died last year."

The crowd stares.

"That's 23 million per day, nearly 300 per second."

Portman kneels beside a woman weeping into her hands.

Tilly continues. "This isn't just factory farms. This is a system of normalized harm."

The heckler stands. "I'm not a factory farm. I do my own processing. People like my friend Maria and I feed our families!"

"Don't forget...they taste damn good," another shouts from the crowd.

Tilly bows her head in silence. Portman joins her on stage. She hands him the mic.

"To the gentleman in the audience..."

The man crosses his arms.

Portman smiles. "St. Francis of Assisi once said, 'Those who exclude any of God's creatures from compassion will deal likewise with their fellow man.'"

Some nods in the crowd.

Portman nods toward a boy in the audience. "That's your son Leif, yes?"

"Yeah, why?"

"Leif, you did a great job showing us your crops the first day."

"Thanks," the boy says.

"Mind if I ask your son a question?"

"You don't have to ask me," the father mutters.

"Leif, what do you think about what Tilly spoke about?"

Max holds the mic for Leif.

The boy says quietly, "I don't like that we kill our animals."

"You like eating them," the father says.

"I don't eat them. I hide the meat in my napkin."

Scattered applause. The father puts his arm around the boy.

"This isn't to shame anyone. Just to ask you to stay." Portman returns the mic.

Tilly takes a deep breath. "Our next presenters are all over 100 years old, including Portman Royal himself. Please welcome our honored Elders."

Applause.

A gray-haired woman walks up the aisle, holding a fluffy, black-faced baby lamb on a leash. Behind her, a tall man with deep wrinkles in Carhartts walks beside a bouncy piglet.

An elderly man rides a three-wheeled trike with a basket full of three chickens, a golden Buff Orpington, a snow-white Rhode Island Red, and a fluffy Chinese Silkie.

Perla guides an elderly person as a teenage boy leads Bruno's favorite miniature Highland calf.

Two geese waddle ahead of an older man. He scoops one up while the other honks and follows.

The crowd laughs.

"Two presenters have walked out," Max says backstage.

"And half the audience," Camas says loudly.

"Not half," Max corrects.

"Close. This was too much," Camas says.

"Camas, you're the queen of too much. We agreed. What's gotten into you?" Max questions.

"I crossed my fingers when we voted," Camas shrugs.

Tilly winces. "How are we going to fill the slots? I'm so sorry, Max."

Bruno appears. "Did I hear you need a speaker?" He offers a hand. "I'm Bruno Die Weisse. Baesamen U.S. I'd be honored to present. Might add some...balance."

Camas scowls. "We don't nee..."

Max interrupts. "Thank you, Bruno. What would your topic be?"

"I promise value, and no 'meaty' topics. I understand your sensitivities."

Tilly straightens. "Can you speak without pushing synthetic methods?"

"Of course, my dear," Bruno answers slowly. "I wouldn't dare."

Portman steps forward. "Mr. Die Weisse, I'm Portman Royal."

They shake hands cooly.

"We can place you in the final slot at 1:30. Fallon Savoreaux walked out."

"1:30 it is." Bruno nods, turns, and leaves.

CHAPTER 27

Empress™ Purple Tomato – Del/Ros1-N

(GMO – NORFOLK PLANT SCIENCES)

"Here's Max to introduce our next speaker, Fanny Beautemp of Blue Shepherdess Fields," Tilly says to the festival audience.

"Not so fast," Camas slurs, "I've got a joke."

Tilly turns her head away from the crowd. She whispers, "You've been drinking already?"

"Of course not," Camas brushes her off. She faces the crowd, puffing out her chest, and steps close to the mic. "What's the difference between a hippie and a burner?"

"I don't know Camas, what's the difference between a hippie and a burner?" Max asks.

"A ticket!" Camas says, laughing hysterically, bending over.

"Please welcome Maximo!" Tilly says again, then leads laughing Camas away. "This way, Phyllis Diller."

"Hello all!" Max calls. "Fanny Beautemp's farm earns money from high-quality Blue Faced Leicester sheep's wool. Her herd also mows and fertilizes almond and walnut orchards and does fire prevention grazing in California's central valley."

Tilly leans in close. "There are loads of press here now. They got wind of the animal presentation. Rein it in, sista. Sit here," she points to a chair. "Don't move! I'll get you a coffee."

Camas puts large sunglasses on, slumps back, lifts her foot onto her knee, and crosses her arms. Camas listens to Max distractedly. Tilly hands her a coffee.

"Are you sure you can introduce Baesamen in your condition? Maybe Max should do it."

"I've got it."

"Make sure you eat lunch."

Camas opens the hotel room door. She pours a small orange juice into a highball glass. She opens three miniature vodka bottles, pours them in, then chugs it. She grabs four more nips of bourbon, shoves them into her backpack, checks her hair in the mirror, then her cell phone, then leaves the room.

Camas orders a beer and a whiskey at the hotel bar. She drinks them down, then moves quickly toward the conference room.

"Camas?" a woman calls from behind.

"Hi, I'm running to get back to the stage," Camas says, still walking.

"I can walk with you. My name is Georgia. I was a nurse for your mom."

Camas stops. "You knew my mom?"

"She was a wonderful woman."

"Thank you."

"I know you're in a hurry, but I just wanted to meet you. Thanks for stopping." The woman hugs Camas, then turns to leave.

"Wait. How did my mom die?"

"You don't know?" the woman asks, surprised.

"Not the specifics."

"Non-Hodgkin's lymphoma."

"Fuck."

"I'm so sorry."

Camas nods and walks slowly. She reaches into her backpack and grabs a small liquor bottle.

Charlie stands by the edge of the stage, looking at his notes.

Bruno comes up from behind. "Just read the exact wording of the announcement," he says gruffly. "You're lucky to stand on stage with me. Quit slouching."

Charlie straightens nervously.

The festival DJ bops his head to the music. Attendees are finishing their lunches, talking, laughing, and networking.

Camas walks onto the stage. She wobbles, then taps forcefully on a water glass with a spoon.

The glass breaks.

The music lowers. Reporters raise their phones to record. Cameramen lift heavy cameras.

"Whoopsie!" Camas puts the spoon down. "Welcome back, everyone!" she shouts. "Please sit your overalls and tie-dye down and listen up! I hope you enjoyed your lunch. We fed you here so we can get going quickly. And we had your plant-based burger buns made from Kumar so you won't fall asleep. Just to be certain, let's dance!"

The DJ pumps up the volume. Camas dances wildly.

"Come on, Tilly!" she calls.

Some in the crowd join. Tilly smiles cautiously, bobbing her head.

The music lowers.

Camas leans into the mic, "Philipe, the scientist, walks into a lab. His coworker, Alfredo, proudly holds up a test tube. 'What is it?' Philipe asks. 'It's weed killer that cures cancer!' 'Bravo, Alfredo! What do you call it?' 'Lymphoma-Sate.'"

Groans. Some shake their heads.

Tilly walks on stage. "Thank you, Camas," she says with raised eyebrows.

Camas leans on a post at the stage's edge.

Tilly announces, "Our next speakers are from Baesamen. Please welcome Bruno Dei Weise, CEO of the Americas, and Agricultural Advisor Charlie Cowscreek."

A few boos.

Tilly exits.

Bruno smiles thinly. "Thank you, Tilly. You may be wondering what the hell a large chemical company is doing here. The answer is... we have an exciting announcement!"

Boos.

"Hey, what about my thank you?" Camas yells.

"Camas, shush," Tilly scolds. "How much did you drink at lunch?"

"I drank lunch."

"Thank you, Camas," Bruno says dryly. "I always appreciate a good herbicide joke."

The crowd quiets.

"But weeds are no joke," he continues. "If we substituted tilling and hand-weeding for herbicides, the result would be $20 billion loss."

Camas shakes her head and steps forward.

Tilly holds her arm. "Camas, no."

"Herbicide use is the most economical means to control weeds. Everyone says no-till will save the planet. How will crops compete if you can't spray?"

Camas grimaces.

"We estimate weed control for organic can be $1,000 per acre, compared to $50 per acre for conventional."

"Till, let me go!" Camas breaks free of Tilly. "Give me that mic!"

Bruno pulls the mic to his chest. "More jokes?" He hides it behind his back.

Camas turns to the DJ. Tilly shakes her head.

Camas holds out her hand. "For the people, brother."

The DJ hands her the mic.

"Ridiculous!" she says. "We all know that ol' College State report on costs per acre. Didn't they receive millions from Baesamen?"

"Well…"

"And you gene-jockey poison-pushers omit the human, animal, and soil costs. You've sucked the nutrients out of our food. A tomato used to taste like a tomato, and three zucchini at Trader Foes didn't come wrapped in plastic!"

Silence.

"Do we make plastic?" Charlie whispers.

"Not much," Bruno mutters.

"Well, someone does, seed savants!"

"I'm just doing my job," Charlie says.

"Well, why don't you help farmers make their soil healthier?!"

"We help farmers grow more crops," Bruno says.

"And self-pollinate, Charlie adds.

Bruno shushes Charlie. "Enough," he growls.

"Enough is right," Camas yells. "Let's destroy the fuzzy fantastical bees forever and Frankenstein some plants that don't need them! Hell, let's grow plants that don't need earth, and we can sit in a plastic bubble and eat in an effin gas mask!"

A chant begins. "Save our seeds. Save our bees."

Bruno advances to a slide of a smiling farming family.

"You say Giddy-Up doesn't stay in the soil. Now it's raining down from the sky. Agent Tangerine, anyone?!"

"Camas…" Max steps closer.

"And Baesamen sells the poison and the cure. Cancer and chemo from the same conglomerate! Mo poison mo better?"

Applause.

"And that baby up there…" Camas pauses, softens. "Tilly is pregnant. I want a baby too."

Tilly and Max glance at each other.

"Congratulations, Tilly," Bruno says flatly.

"But babies have it worst of all!" Camas roars.

She marches towards Bruno. He backs up.

"Scientific studies match pesticides with premies, cancers, brain defects, ADHD, and autism!"

She grabs the mic from him...and the clicker...and throws them down.

Boom. The audience flinches, then applauds. Some stand.

Luxey whistles.

Camas stares at the crowd.

"What are you applauding for?"

Applause fades.

"You all think you're changing the world with your kombucha and fermented cabbage, but we're still following the same model: land equals power."

Beat.

"The only reason we can buy or lease land is because of our white privilege. You're all a bunch of..." Slurring, "self-aggrandizing colonizer offspring! Sacos!"

Gasps. Max groans.

"I'm a saco too. I inherited a farmhouse. I didn't earn it. My ancestors didn't earn it. They took it!"

Tilly walks onto the state. "Camas, that's enough."

Camas raises her fist. "We're god damned sacos. We need to give all this shit back!"

Tilly leads her offstage.

"Save our seeds," the crowd chants.

"I told them, didn't I? Aren't you proud of me, sista?" Camas slurs.

"I have to finish the festival," Tilly says. "Go back to the room."

"I'll take her," Max says.

Charlie and Bruno stand motionless.

A reporter asks, "Did you get all that?"

The cameraman nods.

Tilly walks back to the center of the stage. "Let's let Baesamen finish."

Bruno nods.

Charlie clears his throat. "Baesamen has been your partner for over 100 years. We sell obviate science to eliminate pests and boost yields. We also care about sequestering carbon and are excited to launch our Soil Topological Universal Cash Kernel. 'Kernel' for short. We'll pay you to join... you don't have to change your practices!"

Rumbling from the crowd.

"What's the catch?!" someone shouts.

Charlie scrolls. "Oh, here it is: 'If you are asked, what's the catch? Answer: no catch.'"

Bruno scowls. Then smiles, and stomps off stage.

CHAPTER 28

Broad Breasted White Turkey "Hitchcock"– Born 3 oz. Slaughtered at 22 weeks, 38 lbs. – Hot carcass weight 28 lbs.

(LIFESPAN 2 YEARS DUE TO BREEDING)

Camas lies on a patio recliner next to the conference hotel pool. She has a blanket pulled over her head. A few festival attendees walk past on their way to breakfast. Camas moans softly in hangover pain. She overhears Bruno talking and lifts the blanket to peek out with one eye.

Tilly stands at the window of the hotel restaurant looking out at the hump of sleeping Camas near the pool. She answers a video call from Liam.

"Hey, how are you and P doing?"

"Missing you," Liam responds from a chair on their deck in Sandglass. "P sits on your paddleboard and looks at the driveway, waiting for you. How are you? You sound low."

"I'm missing you both. Can you put P on?"

"P, come!"

Pedro runs up. Liam squats to center Pedro in the video frame.

"Hi buddy," Tilly says weakly. Pedro wags his tail and licks Liam's hand.

"Thanks, I just needed to see my guys," Tilly says.

Liam smiles. He sits back in the chair. "How did the last day go?"

"A disaster. I ruined everything."

"I doubt that."

"Half the conference walked out because we changed the agenda."

Liam looks surprised.

"Then, the biggest pesticide company in the U.S. commandeered the festival."

"A challenge, but probably not the end of the world?"

"There's more."

"OK."

"I let my best friend ruin her life."

Liam listens.

"You know, I've mentioned that Camas has been drinking more than usual. I questioned her about it now and then, but I didn't realize how bad it had gotten. She kind of went off the deep end on stage yesterday."

"You know you can't control someone. That was true with your brother Moore, remember?"

Tilly is silent. Pedro's ears lift on screen.

"Where is she now?" Liam asks.

"She's passed out on a lounge chair near the pool. She didn't even come back to the room last night."

"Shoot."

"I was angry with her, but I'm scared."

"You're a good friend, Till. Camas loves you. I love you too."

"She's my best friend."

"I know. Oh, by the way, Olivier Clan called. He asked me to have you call him."

Cleo runs along a pond of waterlilies, then past a row of colorful food trucks. They see a truck sign that reads *Vegan Va-Jay-Jay's*. The side of the truck features a Georgia O'Keeffe-style vertical rose-colored taco.

Cleo slows, then stops to read the menu: naughty bits $6.50, beef curtains $9, pink tacos $6, magic muffins $4, love tunnel burrito $5. 50, croque mons-sieur $6.

A large man with tattoo sleeves, a L O V E neck tattoo, and a snug white t-shirt over well-developed pecs leans his head down towards the window opening. "What can I getcha, darlin'?"

"I'll have a coffee and the pink tacos, please," Cleo says.

"You got it. That's $8.50."

Cleo pays, then their phone buzzes.

"Where are you?" Bruno demands loudly.

"I'm at Tower Grove Park. It's Saturday."

"You work Saturdays."

"Because you overwork me. I'm not working today."

"You can't just leave me hanging after your text."

The food truck owner hands Cleo the tacos and coffee. A line has formed behind them.

"Thank you," Cleo says. "Hang on, Bruno." They sigh, walk to a bench, and sit down. "OK, I'm back."

"Read it again!"

"It just came over the AP wire. 'California announces moratorium on a list of pesticides for any farms within a specified radius of ground-water recharge areas.'"

"Based on what?"

"It says that they are in a veritable quagmire. The aquifers are going dry, so they need to allow flood waters over farmland to recharge them."

"That's not new. Governor Handsome has been working on that AgMAR for years, and Governor Moonbeam before that."

"I quote, 'The combination of existing aquifer chemicals combined with pesticides creates super-toxic combinations.'"

Bruno grumbles. "We've known about that. Why do you think we put pesticides inside the crops now? Just waiting for the day when they realize they can't spray anymore." He pauses. "Did they actually say super-toxic?"

"Better than megatoxic, I guess. Randy told me you got lambasted during your presentation."

"Yes, but we had huge press when we made the announcement. Hopefully thousands of farmers will see the clip since it was adjacent to Mistress Camomile Tea morphing into a fireball."

"It has been getting a lot of airtime."

"Good. Did you find a celebrity carnivore?"

"I did. His name is Beau Crimson. He has a top podcast... 200 million downloads a month. Big on the carnivore diet."

"He'll do."

"Do what?" Cleo asks.

"I didn't expect they'd go up against meat."

"Aren't we obviating enough with the water and wildlife? Do we have to kill the cows too?"

"You know the numbers."

"I do."

"Well, we're not giving up the $4 billion in pesticide sales for that animal feed production."

"Of course not." Cleo rolls their eyes.

"Set up a meeting with Crimson."

"Got it."

"And one more thing. No, two more. Send me a list of the ten worst bugs in agriculture and the name of an AI graphics expert. There's a new bug in town... and it's going to put an end to pesticide reform."

Bruno taps his phone and heads back into the hotel.

Camas taps her phone to stop recording.

CHAPTER 29

American Chestnut

(ENDANGERED)

"Camas, is that you?" Charlie asks, standing over Camas in the lounge chair.

Camas groans and rolls away, the blanket pulled over her head.

"Let's take a walk," he says.

"Fuck off."

"Camas. It's me. Charlie."

"Charlie who?"

"I know where there is some thick-cut Dubuque Farms bacon."

Camas peaks out of the blanket. "Shit. Hell no. You're the enemy, and I gave up meat."

"No one will know. It's the best bacon in America."

She moans.

"Grease cures a hangover," Charlie adds.

Camas slowly sits up, still wearing yesterday's clothes. Her beanie is askew, curls matted to one side of her face.

Charlie extends a hand. She doesn't take it, but staggers to her feet.

"Let's walk. This way," Charlie says.

They walk in silence. Camas reeks of double-fermented Blaum Brothers bourbon... once aged in barrels, and again in the desert-dry, musty cave of her mouth.

Camas presses her index finger between her eyebrows and squints. "Got aspirin?"

"Nope. Maybe the diner will have some."

"Shit."

"You made quite an impression yesterday."

She shoots him a look and turns and starts to walk the other way.

"Hey, come back. We don't have to talk about that."

Tears brim in her eyes.

"Let's just walk," he says softly.

They follow a quiet road, turn the corner, and cross the street. Charlie holds open the door of an old diner.

The sign on the host stand reads: Breitbach's since 1852 - Iowa's Oldest Diner. Inside, there is wood paneling, blue and white vintage dishes on the walls, and white paper placemats curling slightly at the corners. They sit.

"Welcome, Charlie," a waitress says.

"Hi Lucy."

Camas manages half a waffle with homemade syrup. Charlie scarfs down steak and eggs over hard.

"Don't miss the feed store," Lucy says with a wink. "Lots of plants, baby chicks, and bulbs."

Camas mumbles, "Are you kidding me?"

"It's just a short walk from here. Best view of the Mississippi," Lucy says cheerfully.

"There's the feed store. Let's check it out."

"Tilly's probably wondering where I am."

"I try to stop at the local feed store wherever I go. A little piece of Americana."

"You're such a farm geek, Chas."

They step inside. Charlie greets the clerk, flips through a seed catalog, and buys a packet of daffodil bulbs.

"Let's go," Camas says.

"Just one more thing."

He walks to the back of the store and opens a door. He nods for her to follow.

Inside, metal chairs form a U shape. People sit talking quietly. Two easels stand with hand-lettered banners.

Camas freezes. Her eyes widen. She turns to leave.

"Welcome!" a woman calls gently from across the room.

"Hi," another adds. "Come on in!"

"You're welcome here."

Charlie rests a hand lightly on her arm. His voice is low. "Camas, are you handling your life?"

She doesn't speak. Her hand slips into her jacket pocket and finds the soft, worn surface of the Wham-O hacky sack. She looks at it.

"No," she says.

"One hour."

CHAPTER 30

Shetland Cabbage

(ENDANGERED)

"Olivier! How are you?"

"Tilly! Hello, my dear," Olivier Clan says. "I'm hanging in there for an old professor. Thanks for calling me back."

"Of course. I saw a clip of your gardening course online. Seems like a light topic for you and Harvard. Gardening?"

"It's undergraduate and I'm nearing retirement, so I'm getting a little wilder. You'd be surprised how deep it goes."

"A better title might have included the founding mothers. I can't imagine the mothers and daughters weren't in the garden too."

"Believe me. My students reminded me of that!"

"Oh, good," Tilly laughs.

"Speaking of wild, I caught some of your Slow Earth Food Festival. My daughter encouraged me to watch."

"That's great. Yeah, it was wild there at the end."

"I know I can count on you and Camas to keep things lively. Rolf Lorenz, who interviewed you, watched every minute of it."

"Wow."

"He didn't exactly ace my exam—pulled a C—but he did some remarkable extra credit I think you'll find interesting."

"We enjoyed the interview. He struck me as brainy under the surface. Shoot."

"He wrote a mock report titled *The Hourglass*, addressed to all 50 State Attorneys General. It includes a draft lawsuit against the largest agrochemical and food processing companies."

"Lawsuits regarding pesticides?"

"That's where it gets interesting. Not just injuries from pesticides, but the cost to society of the illnesses from our food system."

"What's the hourglass?"

"Good question. The hourglass refers to the many consumers on one end, the many farmers on the other end, and the tiny choke point in the middle...a few corporations controlling everything."

"The bottleneck."

"Exactly. His report outlines how consolidation has led to mega-control over crop inputs, prices, processing, and even marketing."

"That's a lot."

"Listen to this." Olivier says, reading, "Many nutritionists believe that ultra-processed food is not food. Instead, they are formulations derived from foods, often chemically modified and exclusively for industrial use, containing little or no whole foods and typically en-

hanced with colorings, flavorings, emulsifiers, and other cosmetic ad-
ditives to make them hyper-palatable."

"No wonder more than half our calories come from that junk. And
it's linked to everything... cancer, diabetes, dementia, depression, and
death. I'd love to read it."

"I'll send it over."

"Tell Rolf to get rid of 'mock' and send it to the Attorneys General."

"I already did."

"Thanks for driving," Luxey says, putting on sparkly pink lipstick.

Paignton keeps his eyes on the road. "No problem."

"That was quite a finale."

"Yep."

They ride in silence.

Paignton breaks it. "After all of that, do you still think we should
get rid of the farmland at Sereneway?"

"I think the adults are beyond changing their habits. So, what's the
point if they're not going to engage... other than buy a microgreens
salad at the Sereneway store?"

"Did you see the kids? They were so proud of their vegetables. I
met a lot of kids walking around the festival. Kids aren't entrenched
in their ways."

"True. One little girl made me a daisy chain, and the flowers were
edible."

"Parents care how their kids eat. And young people are worried about the planet. What if we turned the farm into a learning incubator? Kids grow food and earn money from it. Instead of babysitting or mowing lawns...maybe they start a little produce stand."

"What if they would rather scroll in their bedroom?" Luxey scrolls.

"What would have made you want to grow something as a kid?"

"Having a plot next to a cute boy, I guess."

Paignton laughs. "The social aspect."

"Yeah. I also liked to cook. My mom was a horrible cook. If I had better ingredients, I think I would have cooked more."

"A youth farm school and kitchen would be a great amenity for every housing project."

"We could franchise it!"

"Call Ny."

Luxey taps her phone and puts it on speaker between them.

"Hey guys," Ny answers, "Sorry I didn't get to see you before you left."

"Did you hire the contractor for the new houses yet?" Paignton asks.

"Not yet."

Paignton wraps his hand around Luxey's, holding the phone. "Hold off. Luxey and I want to run an idea by you."

Luxey taps to hang up. Paignton keeps a hold of her hand.

Jester's wife, Melanie, leads Peter into their bedroom where Jester lies in bed with an IV and breathing tubes.

"You've looked better," Peter says. "Not much better, but better."

Jester laughs, then coughs. "Come closer." His voice is wheezy. "They're still draining my lungs to keep me alive, but I'm going to pull the plug soon."

Peter puts a hand on Jester's arm.

"I want to see my kids and grandkids."

Peter nods.

"And I wanted to see you, Pete. There's a hell of a lot of cancer in this community. It's a damn shame that when our livelihoods come from a few thousand bushels, and our margins are so damn thin, we're terrified to get out from under the chemical hammer and subsidies."

"Preach," Peter says gently.

Jester coughs. "But that's not why I asked you here. I had some soil tested at an outside lab. The results didn't match Baesamen's."

"Like what?"

"They claimed huge deficiencies, recommending a major chemical application. But the second opinion said those deficiencies were negligible." Jesters starts coughing again.

Melanie walks over. She and Peter exchange a look.

"Got it," Peter says. "Thanks, Jester. I'll check it out."

"Don't tell anyone. My contract says I have to use Baesamen for all of my testing. The bastards'll sue me."

Peter leans in.

"They's sue us," Jester adds, looking lovingly at Melanie.

"OK."

"One more thing."

"Yes, sir."

"I'm sorry I gave you such a hard time about stopping the pesticides. Every spray I used, one bug died, but another popped up... bigger and stronger."

"Yep."

"Isn't it insane? If they'd broadcast after World War II, 'Hey, America, we've got some leftover chemicals...can we spray them on your food?' there would have been a resounding 'hell, no!' yet, here we are."

"Pretty unbelievable. I accept your apology."

They sit quietly.

"Jester," Peter says, "what do you think could get farmers to change?"

"You mean before they're on their deathbeds?" Jester chuckles.

Peter smiles.

"They'd change if they could sell to their communities. I know I would have loved to sell food to Caloose County rather than to India and China. People spend about five percent of their income on food at home. With nearly 26,000 households in Dubuque, that's over $100 million a year. Seems like a chunk of that could keep some farmers afloat."

Peter nods. "You'll be happy to know Charlie's seen the light, too."

"He's a good man. So are you, Pete."

Peter shakes his hand, hugs Melanie, and leaves the hospital room.

CHAPTER 31

Yellow Crooked Neck "Summer Squash" – ZW20

(GMO - MONSANTO COMPANY, ASGROW)

Tilly opens the door to Camas's room at an Iowa women's alcohol recovery center. The room is sparse with two twin beds, two dressers, a small bookshelf, and one plant.

"Hey," Tilly says.

She walks over, sets a bag down on the floor, and hugs Camas. Then sits on the bed.

"Pretty fancy, isn't it?"

"How are you?" Tilly asks.

"I'm OK. I feel like shit, but it's the first time in a long time that it may be good shit."

Tilly grabs her hand. "A nurse at the festival told me she spoke with you before you were on stage with the Baesamen guy…"

"Charlie."

"Yes, with Charlie, and told you the cause of your mom's death. Is that what upset you?"

"I had a hunch about that before I talked with her. A lifetime living under those cropdusters. But that didn't cause my public freak-out. I just have a problem. I'm an alcoholic, it turns out."

Camas's face crumples into tears.

"Oh, Cam, I didn't mean to upset you."

"It's not you," Camas says through tears. "Someone posted a video of my drunk-attack on stage and the adoption was denied."

"Adoption?"

"I wanted to surprise you. Josh and I were going through the adoption process. I really wanted a papoose to play with your papoose." Camas puts her head on Tilly's shoulder. She tries to speak through the sobs, "It makes sense, though, that my shit childhood wouldn't make me a good mother."

"That is absolutely not true. You'll be a great mother. Right now, though, you need to focus on healing. I lost my parents. I can't lose you."

They sit in silence.

"Hey, I almost forgot," Camas says. "Did you catch that podcaster coming in hot and heavy after meat day of the festival?"

"Meat day? Oh, Day Three you mean?"

"Yup. Camas Explosion Day." She pulls out a phone.

"No, I didn't. Where'd you get that? I thought phones weren't allowed in here."

"I traded it for my compass bracelet. I'm sure they'll take it away soon enough. Here it is." Camas points to a photo of a platter of red meat. "Two weeks ago, my plate was screaming in the Colorado mountains, and tonight, he is a delicious elk dinner."

"Screaming?" Tilly says. "That's heartbreaking."

"This dude...Beau Crimson... is a huge social media influencer."

"Oh, that guy."

"They say he's a cultural phenom," Camas says.

Tilly is quiet.

"Sorry to bum you out," Camas says. "I just wanted you to know what we're up against."

"It's OK. It's just that I can picture that magnificent elk in the forest."

The two sit on the bed quietly.

Camas breaks the silence. "He's the leader sheep."

"Huh?"

"Remember the propaganda films from the Board Leaders Of Our Diet narrated by Temple Grandin that were meant to show us the 'good' meat processing plants as part of the Meat Transparency Project?"

"BLOOD, the meat lobby association. Yeah, I remember. They did one on cattle, pigs, lamb, and turkeys." Tilly says.

"Right. And in the sheep one, they used four trained sheep to lead the other sheep off the trucks into the slaughter pens?"

"They wetted their wool and electrocuted them before slitting their throats. Some were still moving," Tilly says quietly.

"Yep. So Beaux's a leader sheep. The traitor sheep who thinks he is so lamb-damb smart because he's getting fed for leading his buddies down the chute to their death."

"Go on," Tilly says, intrigued.

"All the while, the owners of the slaughterhouse and the meat industry are just using him, and he'll be dead like the rest. In Beau Crimson's case, by colon cancer or heart of darkness."

"Even though red meat has been linked to colon cancer, I wouldn't wish that on him," Tilly says softly.

"No limp dick voodoo?"

"No."

"Darn. That reminds me. My recovery group of drunks, Spirited Obstinate Souse, SOS for short, says I'm supposed to have a higher power. Can you teach me to pray?"

"Sure. But you already know how, twirling yogini."

Camas wipes her nose with her sleeve. "I don't think so. If I knew how, I wouldn't be in this hot mess."

"Remember when you were writing your jokes, and I asked you how you do it?"

"Yeah."

"What did you tell me?"

"That I look for the starkest truth. The reality."

"That's right. You told me that when you find the truth in something, people laugh."

"Uh-huh. I need a prayer, though, not an effin joke."

"All you need to do is add a statement of gratitude to the beginning and end of what you already do, and you've got a prayer. The center is the anchor, the truth that your prayer is already answered."

"Show me."

Tilly closes her eyes. Camas follows.

"Great Spirit, I am grateful to be here with my best friend, Camas. I know you are in all things-- the wind, the river, the fire, the sky, the peace that washes over those healing within the walls of this recovery house. And because I know you are in all things, I know you are within me and Camas, the two-legged, the four-legged, the winged, the creeping, and all of nature. The truth of healing and wholeness is here now. We celebrate that truth. I pass the prayer."

Camas opens one eye and sees Tilly's eyes are still closed.

"Thank you, God. My liver is as clean and pure as an organic eggplant in Carmella's garden before her Great Pyrenees Rodolfo pees on it."

Tilly smiles but remains quiet.

"And my mind is as clear as the windshield on my Runabout boat after I spray it with vinegar and water and see the tall peaks of the Selkirks as I feel the lake's spray on my face." She pauses. "I pass my ass. I mean, I pass the prayer."

Tilly laughs. "And we are so thankful for this knowledge of wholeness. We are elated in thanksgiving. We celebrate as though we are four years old, dancing in the living room in our underwear."

Camas chuckles.

"I release the word because it is already done, and say, and so it is."

"And so it is," Camas repeats.

They open their eyes.

"I wish you could stay," Camas says.

"Me too." Tilly glances around. "Kind of."

They laugh.

"What's in the bag?" Camas asks.

"Oh, I almost forgot." Tilly reaches down, lifts the bag, and pulls out four small terracotta pots filled with soil and a paper envelope. "Perla gave me these seeds for you."

"I'll probably kill them."

"You might."

A recovery house nurse walks in. "Time's up."

"I'll see you up in 27 days," Tilly says lovingly. She pulls the Mary statue out of her pocket and sets it on the bedside table. With wet eyes, she hugs Camas and walks to the door.

"Hey, Till."

Tilly turns.

"I had a dream that the twelve steps of Spirited Obstinate Souse solved our food problems."

CHAPTER 32

Atlantic Bluefin Tuna "Mercurial Muriel" – Born larva 3.5mm Slaughtered at 5 years, 130 lbs.

(NATURAL LIFESPAN 40 YEARS, 2,000 LBS.)

Camas sleeps in the dark of her alcohol recovery room. The deep voice of Portman Royal speaks *The Twelve Steps of SOS*.

1. We admitted we were powerless over chemicals and agro-chemical companies — that our farms had become unmanageable.

2. Came to believe that a Power greater than ourselves could restore us to sanity.

3. Made a decision to turn our will and our farms over to the care of Mother Nature as we understood Her.

4. Made a searching and fearless moral inventory of our farm operations.

5. Admitted to Mother Nature, to ourselves, and to another farmer, the exact nature of our wrongs.

6. Were entirely ready to have Mother Nature remove all these destructive practices.

7. Humbly asked Her to remove our shortcomings.

8. Made a list of all species and nature we had harmed and became willing to make amends to them all.

9. Made direct amends to such species and nature wherever possible, except when to do so would injure them or others.

10. Continued to take our farm operation's inventory and when we were wrong promptly admitted it.

11. Sought through prayer and meditation to improve our conscious contact with Mother Nature as we understood Her, praying only for knowledge of Her will for our farm and the power to carry that out.

12. Having had a spiritual awakening as a result of these Steps, we tried to carry this message to farmers and to practice these principles in all our affairs.

Chapter 33

Bradford Watermelon

(Endangered)

**1. We admitted we were powerless
over chemicals and agrochemical companies —
that our farms had become unmanageable.**
*SOS Principle: All humans have a right to food or to produce
it.*

Camas sits in a recovery circle of women. One by one, they speak. A woman with a gravelly voice shares how she drank from the moment her kids left for school. Another confesses she used her son's graduation party as an excuse to start again. When it is Camas's turn, she takes a long breath.

"I lost it," she says. "At the festival finale, I yelled at the crowd. I think some of what I yelled might have been true, but I was wrecked, and honestly, I can't even remember."

Melanie wheels Jester into the coffee shop. He wears oxygen tubes, his tank strapped to the back of his chair. She opens his laptop and places it on the table in front of him. Jester points to the screen. Melanie films it all with quiet steadiness.

A pesticide tanker truck pulls into a dusty yard and slows beside rusted field tanks. A farmer steps out from the barn, face shaded by a wide-brimmed hat. He studies the truck, then shakes his head and waves it away.

**2. Came to believe
that a Power greater than ourselves
could restore us to sanity.**
*SOS Principle: Natural systems must be protected so that they
can produce healthy food.*

An AI graphic artist stitches together digital insect parts on a massive screen. A multi-jawed creature takes shape and buzzes to life. The artist drags the monster over an image of a corn field, then types a command. A simulated swarm floods the screen.

Camas sits at a shaded table with a recovery counselor. Bees visit the lavender and wild sunflowers in a nearby bed. The counselor waits quietly until Camas breaks the silence.

Charlie walks with his black lab through an orchard brimming with cover crop. At the end of the row, he opens his red-and-white '74 Ford F-100 and pulls out a vintage lunch pail. He sits down to eat under an old Oak on a walnut burl bench surrounded by a hedgerow of fox sedge, little bluestem, switch grass, echinacea, bee balm, mountain mint, yarrow, and coreopsis. Three squirrels race down the tree.

Charlie shakes his head. "Dad always said, if you can't spare ten percent for nature–squirrels for the owls, aphids for the lacewings, a weed to tell you what's lacking – you're not a good farmer."

The dog barks in agreement.

3. Made a decision to turn our will and our farms

**over to the care of Mother Nature
as we understood Her.**
***SOS Principle: Humans have a right to safe and nutritious
food.***

Inside a secured room beneath a tribal casino, a chairman and two council leaders open a vault. An architect follows with a stylus and pad. She sketches racks of waterproof seed drawers and shows them the plan. The chairman nods.

Thunder rumbles over a slaughterhouse roof. A man steps from the barn, arms and apron streaked with blood. He looks up to the sky, then down to the cow at his feet. He drops the captive bolt stunner and walks away. At a roadside trough, he washes his face and hands. Then folds his hands over his face and closes his eyes.

Cleo dumps the contents of their desk drawers into a box. Silent Spring lands face-up. They carry the box into Bruno's office, open the book to the chapter A Fable for Tomorrow, and tape it open to the paw of the giant stuffed grizzly bear. Then they walk to Bruno's desk, find his wire-rimmed readers, and set them carefully on the bear's snout.

Chapter 34

Pietrelcina Artichoke

(Endangered)

**4. Made a searching and fearless moral inventory
of our farm operations.**
*SOS Principle: No rules should prevent countries from control-
ling food imports.*

🐾

Max stands in front of the Burning Man Elders in their Moroccan tent on The Playa. He taps a button on his tablet. Behind him, a screen glows:

BOGO Plant-Go!

Buy one ticket, get one free if your party arrives meat-free!"

Elder Rajikaru nods and raises his mate gourd in approval.

167

Peter walks with Jester along a row of pesticide tanks. A dead bird lies limp in the dirt. Jester stops. Peter does too.

Jester nods towards the bird. "You don't notice the graves piling up until you realize there's one with your name on it too."

Camas sits on her bed, writing in her journal. She gets up, waters the seedlings Tilly gave her, then opens her window and breathes deeply. The early light touches the sprouting leaves.

Portman tours Ny through his food commune.

"It's a work in progress," Portman says, "but we harvest enough for the whole community."

Ny picks up a snap pea and takes a bite. "Crunchy. Glad I got it before Duttur did."

They laugh.

5. Admitted to Mother Nature,
to ourselves, and to another farmer,
the exact nature of our wrongs.

SOS Principle: Everyone has a right to information about how their food is produced.

Ny walks Portman around his agrihood, Sereneway.

"This phase has bifacial solar and absorbs sunlight from the underside too," Ny says. "And that house has the mushroom walls I told you about."

Portman nods slowly, taking it in.

Olivier Clan testifies before a Senate subcommittee. A monitor above them reads:

Public Health Ramifications of Agricultural Pesticide Use.

Underneath, a new line fades in:

A Public Trust-Funded Commons for Regenerative Organic Transformation

Jester, in a wheelchair with oxygen tubes, addresses the Caloose Farm Bureau.

"I'm 83 and I have lung cancer. I was never a smoker, but at 42, I was hired as a consultant for Baesamen to plant test fields of their GMO corn in the 80s. That included spraying plenty of Giddy-Up. About two years after the first harvest, I was diagnosed with leukemia."

He pauses a beat. "Maybe if I'd spoken up sooner..." he trails off.

Asa rises to join him. "I lost my son to cancer."

Jester nods. He gestures. The lights dim. A video plays.

Bruno, standing poolside, growls, "Send me a list of the ten worst bugs in agriculture and the name of an AI graphics expert. There's a new bug in town..."

The crowd shifts, murmurs, curses.

Jester leans in. "If we can't lead, let's at least not block the kids who can."

Peter clasps a hand on Charlie's shoulder. A few farmers nod and walk out. A third of the room applauds.

**6. Were entirely ready to have Mother Nature
remove all these destructive practices.**
*SOS Principle: Regions should have the right to regulate their
own agriculture.*

A woman leads Cleo, Paul, Dubs, Hopper, Adofo, and Percy through a high-tech greenhouse. She sketches a greenhouse beside a basketball court, waves painted across the asphalt.

They follow her outside. She points to a new backboard mounted high on the glass wall. They all grin and shake hands.

In Des Moines, a 13-year-old lugs a bin of colorful lettuces into a busy kitchen. A teenage boy follows with bok choy and Thai basil. The Harbinger chef inspects the produce, nods, and signs the invoice.

They trot back to their electric Sereneway van laughing.

A gale tears across bare farmland. Soil lifts into the sky in a thick, choking, dust devil spiral.

CHAPTER 35

BARI Bt Begun-1™ Eggplant

(GMO – Maharashtra Hybrid Seed Company)

7. Humbly asked Her to remove our shortcomings.
SOS Principle: Local production and consumption should be encouraged.

Tilly stands outside a meat processing plant, surrounded by protesters chanting and holding signs. A worker approaching the gate stops. He takes off his work jacket, pulls on a *Mercy for Animals* t-shirt, accepts a sign that reads *Peace on Earth Starts on Your Plate*, and joins the chant.

A crane hoists a new sign onto the upscale Hard Rock Casino restaurant: Council Oak Restaurant covers Council Oak Steakhouse.

Inside, drummers and dancers perform a ceremony as guests at the slot machines and game tables turn to watch. In a nearby meat locker with a viewing window into the casino, carcasses are unhooked and wheeled away. Elders enter with handwoven seed baskets and place them in the center of the drummers. The glass window is cleaned. A wooden cabinet is affixed to it. The seeds are placed gently inside, and dried herbs now hang from the ceiling for healing, cooking, and remembering.

A car pulls up to a farmstand bursting with color -- tomatoes, peppers, squash, melons, plums, walnuts, popping corn, and farm-milled pizza flour. In the distance, a tiny house with flowers in the window overlooks a thriving two-acre plot.

**8. Made a list of all species and nature
we had harmed and became willing
to make amends to them all.**
SOS Principle: Regional biodiversity must be protected.

Camas walks along a creek near the recovery center. Monarch and Orange Sulfur butterflies hover over pink and white Swamp Milkweed. She spreads her sweatshirt on the grass and sits. She pulls a notebook and pen out of her bag and begins writing her amends. She pauses, reaches into her bag and takes out a crumpled hot-pink envelope. She feels it between her fingers. The creases are soft from weeks in the bag.

Want to read the letter Camas found? Download the free short story "Dear Camas Lily" (with a peach shortcake recipe) at aviskalfsbeek.co m/camaslily.

A young farmer pulls up to a drive-through window at the Winstar Casino. He hands over a card and receives a printed ticket. Around the back at the loading dock, a worker loads a sack of heritage seed into his truck bed.

"Gambling today, Joe?" the worker teases, nodding toward the glittering megacasino.

"Nope, not anymore," Joe grins. "I'm selling local now. No more market roulette. I mill my own grain. Even the casino bakery buys some." He pats the seed sack. "Turns out, I'm an artisan."

"Cool!"

They shake hands.

Portman Royal guides the hand of an 11-year-old girl as she shears a Rambouillet sheep, brow furrowed with focus. A tattooed sheep farmer steadies the animal between her knees while the tufts of wool fall to the ground. The girl hands the sheers to the farmer, who finishes the last strokes and gently releases the sheep. All three laugh as it bounds back toward the flock in the open grass.

**9. Made direct amends to such species and nature
wherever possible, except when to do so
would injure them or others.**
SOS Principle: Seeds are a "common property" resource.

Josh arrives at the recovery center. Camas steps out with her panniers, eyes bright. He rushes to her. She drops her bags. He kisses her firmly. They hold each other.

At the Napa Farmer's Market, a young man in an apron blends a smoothie with kale, mint, baby bok choy, spinach, romaine, mango, banana, and a smile. Next door, the Conservation District booth reads Free Bee Boxes and Free Owl Boxes.

Charlie chops onions in the farmhouse kitchen. Peter shows him how to shape black bean patties as his mother sets a vase of zinnias on the table.

At a desert festival booth, a man with his hair tied up in a bun shows his phone to a young woman in yoga pants and a glittering belly-dance hip scarf.

Buy One Get One Free ticket to Burning Man 2025
for attendees who enter meat-free
and sign the Flesh-Free Pledge.
(Value $800 per free ticket.)

Barred Plymouth Rock Heritage Chicken "Gertie" – Born 1 lb. Slaughtered at 20 weeks, 8 lbs. – Hot carcass weight 6 lb.

(NATURAL LIFESPAN 8 YEARS)

10. Continued to take our farm operation's inventory
and when we were wrong
promptly admitted it.
SOS Principle: No life form should be patented, and termina-
tor seeds should be banned globally.

Two workers take down a sign reading *Faaberg's Hog Farm* at the farm's entrance. A tall white hay barn, two long and low rectangular structures, and assorted outbuildings stand in the distance. They screw the new sign up, place a level on top, tighten the screws, then stand back to admire their work.

"*1100 Mushroom Farm,*" one of the workers reads aloud. "What's the 1100?"

"That's how many hogs those barns held before they went to slaughter. He doesn't want to forget."

Charlie hammers a For Sale sign into the ground beside a rusty tractor tiller and a pesticide spray rig near Camas's Iowa farmhouse. The sign reads:

For Sale $1 million each.
Organic Peaches U-Pick $1.50 / lb, We Pick $2.50 / lb.

From the passenger seat of his pickup, Jester watches a farmworker raise a painted sign beside a lush cover crop of peas, oats, turnips, and radishes. It reads:

One- to Five-Acre Parcels For Lease
New Organic and Regenerative Farmers
Water, Electricity, and Equipment Share Available.
He leans over to kiss Melanie.

11. Sought through prayer and meditation to improve our
conscious contact with Mother Nature
as we understood Her, praying only for knowledge
of Her will for our farm and the power to carry that out.
SOS Principle: Freedom to exchange seeds should be protected.

Joss parks the van in front of a corner market in a Los Angeles food desert. She unloads boxes of vegetables and hands them to the shopkeeper. Her name tag reads Volunteer—Joss, and the van is painted with cheerful stripes and the words *Nutritious Neighbor Hood*.

Joss sits across the table from a bearded podcaster in a sleek studio. A matte-black device stands upright on a square charger.

"You've had extreme success with your Veg-Health Meter, Joss. Why the expansion to meat?"

"Huge demand," she says, smiling

"What does it test?"

"Pathogens, pesticides, antibiotic drug residues, and heavy metals."

"Such as?"

"Sure. Pathogens like E. coli, Salmonella, Listeria, Clostridium, Staph, Campylobacter, Bacillus, and Shigella. Pesticides like Glyphosate and other organophosphates."

"Easy for you to say."

Joss laughs. "The device also detects antibiotic residues and traces of industrial runoff metals."

"Sounds...appetizing," the host quips.

"Consumers have a right to know."

"How much?" Rich asks.

"About what you'd pay for mid-range headphones."

"Thirty bucks?"

"Right around there."

He laughs and pulls the device from his pocket. "My wife loves it."

"Fantastic!"

'But your veggie investors didn't fund the meat version?"

"Nope. Many were vegetarian and didn't want to enable meat sales. Others believed the meter would actually stop people from eating meat altogether."

"Do you think it will?"

Joss smiles, "I'm not able to comment on that."

12. Having had a spiritual awakening as a result of these Steps, we tried to carry this message to farmers, and to practice these principles in all our affairs.
SOS Principle: Farmers should have the right for their land to be free of genetic contamination.

A community garden flourishes on the edge of the Project Backboard court. Cleo teaches a seed-starting group. Zaria kneels beside a younger child, showing how to tuck a seedling into the soil. Paul calls out the build instructions for a high tunnel greenhouse. Hopper, Percy, and four volunteers assemble it beside the court. Adofo and Dubs play one-on-one nearby.

Across the country, three teens sit at a crumbling urban court, eyes fixed on a phone. On screen, Cleo teaches the class. The court behind them is overgrown and cracked. They laugh at Cleo's plant jokes.

Charlie and Peter lead a tour through an abundant organic peach orchard. Cover crop blankets the center rows. A white splatter lands on Peter's forehead. He wipes it with his sleeve and examines it.

"Recycled insects," he says, smiling.

The group laughs.

"I hear that's good luck," Charlie says.

Tilly steps off the train in Sandglass. Liam and Pedro are waiting.

Liam kisses her face. Pedro licks her face.

Tilly laughs and holds them both.

CHAPTER 37

Ele Ele "Black Hawaiian" Banana

(ENDANGERED)

Tilly sits with Frida at the peace rock in the mountains above Sandglass.

"Why do I feel so powerless?" Tilly asks.

"Is that how you truly feel?"

"Our food is poisoned. Our waters are poisoned." Tilly's voice is pained. "Our leaders listen to those who give them money for their political campaigns, those selling death, not life, so how can things be different? I don't see a clear path."

"Maybe you can't see the path because it is an ocean, not a river."

Tilly considers.

Frida stands. "Come with me."

Tilly follows.

Frida picks up a stick and walks to the fire circle. In the cool ashes, she draws a large circle, its diameter equal to her height. She draws two lines within the circle, north to south and east to west.

"What do you see?"

"A medicine wheel," Tilly answers.

Pedro runs around the hill behind them. He looks up at a butterfly, then trots to a nearby tree and back to Tilly.

"P, lie down."

Pedro obeys. Frida and Tilly look at the wheel.

"You've shared some hopeful things from your journey. Where would you place these on the medicine wheel?" Frida asks, handing Tilly the stick.

"I don't know what you're asking of me."

"You told me that children make you hopeful. That you heard of a plan to make schools for children to learn to grow and sell food."

Tilly closes her eyes. She opens them, then walks around the circle in the ashes. She places the end of the stick where the line meets the circle to the east.

"The sun rises, the beginning of a new day, with the light of wisdom and understanding. This is the hope of children."

She writes *children* in the ashes.

"And to the south?" Frida asks.

"The sun is at its highest. There is warmth, things growing. The life of all things comes from the south. This is the hope of large communities of people growing their own food."

Tilly writes *cities and towns* in the ashes at the bottom of the circle.

"And to the west?"

"The sun sets. The day ends. The west is rain, lakes, streams, and rivers. The water flows."

Tilly writes *native seed banks* in the ashes at the western point of the wheel.

"And to the north?"

"The north teaches us to face the cold, harsh winds of winter with cleansing winds. Like a buffalo standing headfirst into a storm, she has learned endurance."

Tilly writes *farmers* in the ashes at the north.

Frida pulls a pouch from her pocket and hands it to Tilly. Then she begins to sing a beautiful chant. The sounds float over Pedro's curls, through the wild syringa and beargrass, into the leaves of the pine and white spruce.

Tilly opens the pouch and pours the contents into her palm. She smiles at the colorful seeds and Frida, then pours them back into the pouch. She holds it in both hands, blessing them.

She gently places the pouch in the center of the medicine wheel. With the stick, she writes *seeds* at the center.

Frida's heart song ends.

Tilly picks up the pouch and hands it to Frida.

Frida closes her eyes for a moment, then places it back into Tilly's hands.

Tilly looks up. "I had a dream about this... you putting this seed pouch in my hands."

Frida smiles softly. "I'm sure you did."

Tilly feels her baby kick.

Three generations of Native women, and a curly canine, move down the hill as a light rain begins to fall, and the medicine wheel melts back into the earth of the ancient fire circle.

CHAPTER 38

Lemon Cling Peach

(ENDANGERED)

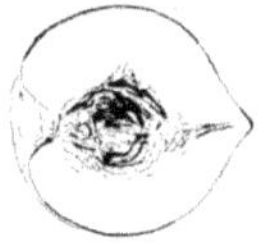

Tilly and Liam drive up to Camas's farmhouse and honk the horn.

Camas walks out wearing a light blue kaftan, her strawberry blond curls falling onto her sun-kissed face, which brightens into a wide smile at the sight of her best friend.

Tilly gets out of the car, holding the car door as she squeezes her nine-and-a-half-month pregnant belly through.

"Wow, look at this!" she says, hugging Camas. "The place looks great!"

The farmhouse gleams with a fresh coat of white paint. Flower boxes of red geraniums hang from the windowsills.

"I know, huh. A bit different from when we first got here. Wow, look at your belly!" Camas hugs Liam. "Josh is inside," she tells him. "I'm so happy you two are here."

"So are we," Liam says.

"Sit," Camas motions to a light teal Adirondack chair on the porch. A Joseph's Coat rose with cherry-red, deep gold, and orange petals climbs the porch frame.

"So, are you keeping the farmhouse?" Tilly asks.

"I'm keeping it, but after the wedding, we're coming back to Sandglass."

"Whew, thank goodness," Tilly smiles.

"I've got One More Year to run, you know."

"Yes, I know."

"Charlie's leasing the farmhouse and converting the peach orchards and land to regenerative organic. He and his dad are going to hold classes for farmers – newbies and old geezers alike."

"So we'll be able to eat the peaches!"

"You got it. He'll be growing a whole bunch of other things, too. I was thinking. We should add a rooftop garden to the boathouse when we get back to Sandglass."

"Sounds great. I missed you, Cam. It's so good to see you. You look beautiful."

"I always look fabulous," Camas says, squeezing Tilly's hand.

"Yes, you do," Tilly laughs and squeezes back.

Camas looks out over the lawn. "I made amends to my dad and stepmom, but they still aren't coming to the wedding. I could apologize for my drinking behavior, but not for the color of my love's skin."

"Got it."

"I want to make amends to you. And living amends to my mom."

"No amends are needed here, sista."

"Till, I'm sorry for my drinking, the times I made you worry, the times I left you in the lurch."

"Thank you. I accept your apology," Tilly says warmly.

A tall man with smiling eyes and a salt-and-pepper beard strums sweet ukulele music on the porch. About sixty guests -- the Bike Guys, Peter and Charlie, farm workers, Cashal, a few locals, and friends of Camas's mother -- mingle on the lawn.

Max walks to the edge of the walkway and pulls the chain of an antique farm bell. Guests settle into chairs underneath a thick canopy of peach tree branches.

Josh and Liam stand at the end of the aisle beside Max, all dressed in elegant, colorful Indian vestments.

Camas descends the farmhouse steps in a light peach-colored chiffon mini-dress, white lace platform boots, and a knee-length white veil embroidered with pink beads. She carries a bouquet of peach, orange, gold, and hot pink zinnias in one hand and a vintage metal Pokémon *Gotta Catch 'Em All* case in the other, containing her mother's ashes.

Tilly follows her down the stairs. Camas hands her the case.

The ukulele music shifts into a Hawaiian-esque *Here Comes the Bride.*

Tilly and Camas join hands and walk down the aisle. At the front, Tilly kisses Camas on the cheek, then places the Pokémon case on a seat in the front row.

Camas turns to Josh. They smile, then face Max.

Tilly and Liam stand beside them.

Camas and Josh exchange vows with giggles and tears.

Max offers words of hope, love, and forever. "You may kiss the bride."

Camas places her hand on Josh's back and dips him into a long, romantic dance-move kiss.

The crowd bursts into laughter and applause.

They rise, kiss again, then hug Tilly and Liam.

Tilly's water breaks.

CHAPTER 39

New Leaf Plus™ Russet Burbank Potato

(GMO – J.R. Simplot Company)

Josh, Camas, Tilly, and Liam sit in low chairs around a wooden coffee table in Matchlove Brewery. Liam bounces a baby on his knee. Pedro lies on the ground and looks up as the baby starts to cry. Liam passes the baby to Tilly, who drapes a blanket over her shoulder to breastfeed.

Josh raises a beer glass. "Here's to Camas and me being approved as foster parents!"

"What?!" Liam and Tilly say in unison.

Pedro barks.

"That's so wonderful!" Tilly says.

"I won't be able to pull my boobs out in public as a foster parent, but we are so happy!" Camas says, raising her non-alcoholic IPA.

"You know you never need an excuse to pull your breasts out," Tilly teases.

They all laugh.

A large screen hangs over the beer taps. A reporter appears on-screen, standing at the edge of a wheat field as a harvester moves behind him.

Tilly points. "Shush -- listen!"

The reporter announces, "The $400 billion lawsuit filed by all 50 State Attorneys General against Baesamen, Syndown, and 98 other agrochemical companies – collectively known as the Agrochemical Processed Foods Master Settlement Agreement – has settled. In a rare show of unity, the case accused these corporations of colluding to steal seeds from nature, mutate them for private gain, and cause public harm through pesticides, processed foods, and pharmaceutical dependencies created by their own products."

The feed cuts to a courtroom: executives hunched beside lawyers, working men and women sitting behind them.

"If upheld, this will be the largest lawsuit in history, surpassing the 1998 Tobacco Master Settlement Agreement of $206 billion. Half of the funds will be designated for community farming and truth-in-food initiatives nationwide."

Tilly buttons her top. She and Camas stand up and hug, eyes still wide as they turn back to the screen.

"Some have questioned how this settlement could exceed tobacco's. Here's Harvard Law professor Olivier Clan."

Olivier Clan appears on screen, calm and composed. "The cost of planetary harm, soil degradation, ecosystem collapse, and the medical fallout of chemically manipulated food is astronomical. The agrochemical sector's entanglement with Big Pharma creates a self-perpetuating profit loop. At a valuation of $1.6 trillion, these companies can afford this. Frankly, I wonder if the settlement is too low."

Bruno hammers his boxing bag in his office. The spectacled grizzly lounges in the corner, reading Silent Spring. The TV blares in the background.

"...the $400 billion lawsuit filed by all 50 State Attorneys General against Baesamen, Syndown..."

Bruno lies in a hospital bed, scrolling his phone. Cleo enters with a gift bag.

"I'll call you back," Bruno mutters, ending the call.

"Hey. You OK?" Cleo asks.

"Do you care?"

"I do. I brought you cookies and Killepitsch."

Bruno uncorks the red liqueur, pops the lid off a plastic hospital cup, and pours. He sips through the straw. "How's the basketball sharecropping?"

Cleo sighs. "They're urban basketball farms. We call them Farm Courts."

"Yeah, those."

"We've opened ten. Another fifty are in planning for next year."

"Maybe you'll need some products."

"Nope. The farms are organic."

"We're rebranding some things that might work. 'Natural.' 'Biological.' 'Activating' instead of 'obviating,' that sort of thing."

"Hmmm."

They sit in silence.

"Come back to work for me," he says.

"No, I can't do that. I just wanted to check on you. You don't look too worried, actually."

Bruno shrugs. "We still have the cows."

Holstein-Friesian "Mame" – Born 90 lbs. Slaughtered at 4 years, 1,500 lbs. – Hot carcass weight 884 lbs.

(NATURAL LIFESPAN 20 YEARS)

A bluegrass band plays in the park as people bustle through the Sandglass Farmers' Market. The trio sings,

"We'll build a home. We'll start a family.

We'll till the garden.

Won't run away if it starts to rain.

We'll till the garden.

We'll harvest til we are wrinkled, old, and gray."

Nasturtiums float in herbed iced tea and are woven into the tea maker's braided hair. The smells of lavender and orange oils, hand-made soaps, and freshly baked bread drift through the air.

Liam holds Pedro's leash as he and Josh watch the band.

Tilly and Camas sit on a bench at the edge of the market. Two one-year-old toddlers play on the grass in front of them.

"Till, Josh, and I are going to pick up dinner stuff," Liam says. "We can take the kids."

"Thanks, honey. We're out of olive oil and hummus. I'll hold P."

Liam hands Tilly Pedro's leash. He lifts a small red-haired girl with olive-toned skin into a stroller. Josh picks up his foster son -- a Black toddler with a beanie, fat arm rolls, and a beaming smile -- and buckles him in.

Liam kisses Tilly, Josh kisses Camas, then they wheel the strollers off towards the vegetable stalls.

The music continues:

"We'll shower in graces of wholehearted embraces,
of our past, our future, and our children's faces.
Feast on the table, the cat's on the sill,
warm light pours through the windows.
Our long lives fulfilled. Hey."

"I still can't get over that you have a red-haired baby," Camas says.

"Just like her auntie," Tilly smiles. "Probably from Liam's side, but who knows?"

"Horizontal gene transfer," Camas says, tapping her strawberry blond curls.

They laugh, watching the parade of passersby.

"I had a dream last night that Bruno Die Weise got fired and went totally crazy," Camas says.

"You mean crazier? I heard he had a full-on breakdown. I feel sorry for him."

"In my dream, he was walking through a corn maze the size of Iowa in a giant monster bug costume."

"Sounds like a video game. Mono Mutante?"

Up ahead, Josh and Liam walk side by side, chatting as they push the strollers.

Tilly points, "Look. They're holding hands!"

"The guys?" Camas deadpans.

The toddlers sit in their strollers, little hands linked between them.

Camas stands up. "Come on. Let's make sure they don't forget the potatoes."

THE END

Pedro's Primer

Tilly asked me to share a few woofs with you.

One day I was on a walk with Tilly and I got the zoomies. You know that feeling you get when you can't contain your happiness and you run as fast as you can, stop on a dime, then turn around and run at top speed in the opposite direction, then repeat? Or, sometimes, you run in circles because your tail is just out of reach. It was one of those days. I ran fast, faster, fastest! The dust from the field rose around me and I thought I might burst from happiness!

Then, I heard Tilly shout, "P! Stop! Come!"

I stopped.

"Sorry, buddy. We can't play in that dirt. My friend told me it's full of poison."

"Woof!" I answered.

I love poi and sun, I thought to myself. We had both of those at a luau in Hawaii. I started racing in a circle again, faster and faster.

"P, no!!"

I saw from the look on her face, she meant business. I stopped. I obeyed and joined her on the path next to the field.

Even if I don't know what poison is, I'm thinking that if I'm not allowed to run around in it, maybe you shouldn't eat fruit or veggies grown in it either.

I sure hope the birds, bees, mice, deer, and other dogs have moms to warm them to stay out of there.

People think I eat vegan dog food because I'm not smart or because my mistress Tilly is a hippie. That's not why. It's because cows are my friends.

Woof.

P

PEDRO DE SOUSA SARAMAGO MEGELLAN

Also By Avis Kalfsbeek

Avis

BOOKS

One More Year

A Pedro the Water Dog Saves the Planet Primer 1

Plastic Plankton

A Pedro the Water Dog Saves the Planet Primer 2

Bike Rock

A Pedro the Water Dog Saves the Planet Primer 3

Copper Cobra

A Pedro the Water Dog Saves the Planet Primer 4

Planeteering

A Pedro the Water Dog Saves the Planet Primer 5

AUDIO

Peace is Here Podcast *with Avis Kalfsbeek*

Audio Books Coming Soon!

The Twelve Steps of SOS

Selling Obviate Science, Save Our Seeds, Seeds Over-Soul, Spirited Obstinate Souse

1. We admitted we were powerless over chemicals and agrochemical companies — that our farms had become unmanageable.

2. Came to believe that a Power greater than ourselves could restore us to sanity.

3. Made a decision to turn our will and our farms over to the care of Mother Nature as we understood Her.

4. Made a searching and fearless moral inventory of our farm operations.

5. Admitted to Mother Nature, to ourselves, and to another farmer, the exact nature of our wrongs.

6. Were entirely ready to have Mother Nature remove all these destructive practices.

7. Humbly asked Her to remove our shortcomings.

8. Made a list of all species and nature we had harmed, and became willing to make amends to them all.

9. Made direct amends to such species and nature wherever possible, except when to do so would injure them or others.

10. Continued to take our farm operation's inventory and when we were wrong promptly admitted it.

11. Sought through prayer and meditation to improve our conscious contact with Mother Nature as we understood Her, praying only for knowledge of Her will for our farm and the power to carry that out.

12. Having had a spiritual awakening as a result of these Steps, we tried to carry this message to farmers, and to practice these principles in all our affairs.

After the Last Bite

A Post-Credits Coda to Mono Mutante

CAST:

Soil and Seed

Tim Parton (Breward Park Farm)

Wendell Berry

Rachel Carson (1907 – 1964)

John Kempf

Cicero (106 – 43 BC)

Jason Gerhardt (Permaculture Institute)

Mahatma Gandhi (1869 – 1940)

Robin Wall Kimmerer

Bees and Bites

Willa Honeypot (fictional, USDA sourced)

Chef Babette Davis

Captain Paul Watson

Camas (fictional, Mono Mutante)

Jeremy Bentham (1748 – 1832)

Isaac Bashevis Singer (1903 – 1991)

Meat and Mind

George Bernard Shaw (1856 – 1950)

Ralph Waldo Emerson (1803 – 1882)

Michael Pollan

Socrates (470 – 399 BC)

Glaucon (445 – 4th century BC)

Peace and Philosophers

Henry David Thoreau (1817 – 1862)

Henry Stephen Salt (1851 – 1939)

Lancelet (fictional, The Merchant of Venice)

Leonardo Da Vinci (1452 – 1519)

EXT. DUBUQUE BOTANICAL GARDENS – DAY

A quiet path winds through native blooms. TIM PARTON, RACHEL CARSON, JOHN KEMPF, CICERO, WENDELL BERRY, JASON GERHARDT, MAHATMA GANDHI, ROBIN

WALL KIMMERER, and WILLA HONEYPOT stroll in the sun, stopping to observe bees, soil, and petals.

TIM PARTON

I haven't applied NPK fertilizers for 10 years now so that's a massive savings on my farm.

JOHN KEMPF
(to CICERO)
Nitrogen, phosphorus, potassium.

TIM PARTON

That's 20 - 30 thousand pounds straight away. I'm not buying as much nitrogen. I'm not spending 100 pounds per hectare on fungicides. I'm not spending the money on herbicides. The little bit I spend on nutrition is still far far less than what I'm spending on all these synthetic horrible products that are just killing everything. We've got herbicides. We've got fungicides. We've got insecticides and to me, the three things they've got in common is suicide to us as a society.

JOHN KEMPF

I see no consumer demand for tasteless strawberries.

CICERO

Of all the occupations from which gain is secured, there is none better than agriculture, nothing more productive, nothing sweeter, nothing more worthy of a free human.

AVIS KALFSBEEK

WENDELL BERRY

The grower of trees, the gardener, the human born to farming, whose hands reach into the ground and sprout, to them the soil is a divine drug.

JASON GERHARDT

We don't cure our crisis of culture and humanity without coming back to the land. We have to become Indigenous to our place and each other. That is permaculture.

JOHN KEMPF

When we embrace responsibility, I see people's lives be so strongly associated with finding joy. Over and over, farmers tell us that they're having fun. It's so rewarding to engage in this process of co-creation with natural ecosystems.

MAHATMA GANDHI

To forget how to dig the Earth and tend the soil is to forget ourselves.

ROBIN WALL KIMMERER

The plants can tell us her story; we need to learn to listen.

A butterfly lands on CICERO's shoulder. The group pauses, smiling.

WILLA HONEYPOT

Thank animal pollinators for one of every three bites of food you take. Bees, butterflies, moths, birds, bats, beetles and other insects. 3,500 species of native bees help increase crop yields. In North America, neonicotinoid insecticides were found in 86% of honey samples. Managed honey bee colonies in the U.S. dropped from five million in the 1940s to about two and a half million in 2023.

RACHEL CARSON

Can anyone believe it is possible to lay down such a barrage of poisons on the surface of the Earth without making it unfit for all life?

EXT. HOTEL POOL AND PING PONG TABLES - DAY

Bright umbrellas shade a pool deck. CAMAS, CHEF BABETTE, ISAAC BASHEVIS SINGER, and JEREMY BENTHAM play doubles. CAPTAIN PAUL WATSON wades in the pool with sunglasses and clipboard.

Across the deck, four SUITED MEN order cocktails, ribeye, ahi steak, and double-patty cheeseburgers.

CHEF BABETTE
(glancing at the meat-laden table, swings, misses)
Darn it. I don't believe in killing animals to nourish yourself. You don't have to give up anything in your food. Just... death.

CAPTAIN PAUL WATSON

We go where others fear to go, no matter how hostile or remote the seas, no matter how formidable the opposition because if we don't, life in the seas dies and if the ocean dies, we die.

CAMAS

(picking up the ping pong ball near the SUITED MEN's table, walks back with a sexy swagger)

Besides the tomahawk, they've got fish too. Is fish OK?

JEREMY BENTHAM

(resets the serve)

Camas, tomahawk is not P.C.

CAMAS

Sorry.

JEREMY BENTHAM

The question is not can they reason? Nor, can they talk? But, can they suffer?

ISAAC BASHEVIS SINGER

(slams a fast shot over the net)

As long as human beings will go on shedding the blood of animals, there will never be any peace. There is only one little step from killing animals to creating gas chambers à la Hitler and concentration camps à la Stalin.

INT. SPAM MUSEUM, DUBUQUE - DAY

Bright yellow walls, cans of Spam stacked floor to ceiling. Photos of casseroles and retro kitchens.

GEORGE BERNARD SHAW
(staring at a wall that reads *How many SPAM cans tall are you?*)
Bloody hell. I'm 25 cans of Spam tall. The worst sin towards our fellow creatures is not to hate them, but to be indifferent to them: that's the essence of inhumanity.

RALPH WALDO EMERSON
You have just dined, and however scrupulously the slaughterhouse is concealed in the graceful distance of miles, there is complicity.

MICHAEL POLLAN
Our own worst nightmare such a place may well be; it is also real life for the billions of animals unlucky enough to have been born beneath these grim steel roofs.

EXT. SPAM MUSEUM - BRONZE SCULPTURE OF TWO PIGS & FARMER - DAY

SOCRATES and GLAUCON sit back-to-back on two bronze pigs, gazing at the bronze farmer.

SOCRATES
Would this habit of eating animals not require that we slaughter animals that we knew as individuals, and in whose eyes we could gaze and see ourselves reflected, only a few hours before our meal?

GLAUCON
This habit would require that of us.

EXT. HOTEL POOL - DAY

Feet in the water: CAMAS, HENRY DAVID THOREAU, HENRY STEPHEN SALT, LANCELET, and LEONARDO DA VINCI. CAPTAIN PAUL WATSON wades in the water.

HENRY DAVID THOREAU
I have no doubt that it is a part of the destiny of the human race, in its gradual improvement, to leave off eating animals, as surely as the savage tribes have left off eating each other, when they came in contact with the more civilized.

HENRY STEPHEN SALT

If it can be shown that men can live equally well without flesh-food, or, rather, unless it can be shown that the contrary is the case (for the burden of proof must always rest with those who take on themselves the responsibility of wholesale slaughter), it must surely seem unjustifiable, on the score of humanity, to breed and kill animals for merely culinary purposes.

LANCELET

Truth will come to light; murder cannot be hid long.

LEONARDO DA VINCI

Animals will be seen upon the earth who will always be fighting with one another, with very great losses and frequent deaths on each side. And there will be no end to their malice; ... when they are filled with their food, the satisfaction of their desires will be to deal death, and grief and labor and fear and fright to every living thing; ...And their bodies will become the tomb and the means of transit of all the living bodies they have killed. O Earth! What delays thee to open and hurl them headlong into the deep fissures of a huge abyss and caverns, and no longer to display in the sight of heaven so savage and ruthless a monster?

CAMAS
(holding up a french fry)
Damn, LDV. That's heavy. French fry?

LEONARDO DA VINCI
(takes the fry)
Grazie.

THE END

Percy Schmeiser's Principles for Food and Agriculture

- All humans have a right to food or to produce it.

- Natural systems must be protected so that they can produce healthy food.

- Humans have a right to safe and nutritious food.

- No rules should prevent countries from controlling food imports.

- Everyone has a right to information about how their food is produced.

- Regions should have the right to regulate their own agriculture.

- Local production and consumption should be encouraged.

- Regional biodiversity must be protected.

- Seeds are a "common property" resource.

- No life form should be patented, and terminator seeds should be banned globally.

- Freedom to exchange seeds should be protected.

- Farmers should have the right for their land to be free of genetic contamination.

Percy and Louise Schmeiser were awarded the Right Livelihood Award, known as the "Alternative Nobel Prize," for their courage in defending biodiversity and farmers' rights and challenging the environmental and moral perversity of current interpretations of patent laws (2007).

Percy Schmeiser was inducted into the Canadian Health Food Association Hall of Fame in regard to the awareness of GMOs and their effects on Human Health (2014).

Percy and Louise Schmeiser both received the Environmental Justice award in regard to the dangers of contamination of Indigenous seeds in Peru, Bolivia, Argentina, and the United States (2014).

Hamatreya

BY RALPH WALDO EMERSON

Bulkeley, Hunt, Willard, Hosmer, Meriam, Flint
Possessed the land which rendered to their toil
Hay, corn, roots, hemp, flax, apples, wool, and wood.
Each of these landlords walked amidst his farm,
Saying, "'Tis mine, my children's, and my name's.
How sweet the west wind sounds in my own trees!
How graceful climb those shadows on my hill!
I fancy these pure waters and the flags
Know me, as does my dog: we sympathize;
And, I affirm, my actions smack of the soil."

Where are these men? Asleep beneath their grounds:
And strangers, fond as they, their furrows plough.
Earth laughs in flowers, to see her boastful boys
Earth-proud, proud of the earth which is not theirs;

Who steer the plough, but cannot steer their feet
Clear of the grave.

They added ridge to valley, brook to pond,
And sighed for all that bounded their domain.
'This suits me for a pasture; that's my park;
We must have clay, lime, gravel, granite-ledge,
And misty lowland, where to go for peat.
The land is well,—lies fairly to the south.'
'Tis good, when you have crossed the sea and back,
To find the sitfast acres where you left them.'
'Ah! the hot owner sees not Death, who adds
Him to his land, a lump of mould the more.
Hear what the Earth says:—

EARTH-SONG.
'Mine and yours;
Mine, not yours.
Earth endures;
Stars abide—
Shine down in the old sea;
Old are the shores;
But where are old men?
I who have seen much,
Such have I never seen.

'The lawyer's deed
Ran sure,

In tail,
To them, and to their heirs
Who shall succeed,
Without fail,
Forevermore.

'Here is the land,
Shaggy with wood,
With its old valley,
Mound, and flood.
But the heritors?--
Fled like the flood's foam,
The lawyer, and the laws,
And the kingdom,
Clean swept herefrom.

'They called me theirs,
Who so controlled me;
Yet every one
Wished to stay, and is gone.
How am I theirs,
If they cannot hold me,
But I hold them?'

When I heard the Earth-song,
I was no longer brave;
My avarice cooled
Like lust in the chill of the grave.

Be Part of the Pack

If this book made you smile (or think), please leave a quick review on Amazon or Goodreads — it really makes a difference!

Find more stories, updates, and community at www.AvisKalfsbeek.com

Yours in peaceful love of the planet,

A Final Tail Wag

PEDRO'S HAIKU

Dirt beneath my paws,

Spuds asleep in warm silence...

Sunlight on my nose.